Two-Faced Death

Roderic Jeffries

Table of Contents

CHAPTER I

The telephone rang, waking Alvarez. He shook his head, opened his eyes, and stared balefully at the telephone, willing it to be quiet. It went on ringing and eventually he sat up, reached out, and picked up the receiver.

'This is the office of Superior Chief Salas,' said a woman, very incisive of tone. 'Señor Salas wishes to speak to you.'

One of the shutters, insecurely latched, was slowly swinging outwards and harsh sunshine spilled across the desk. He blinked rapidly and rubbed his eyes. What the hell was the time? He looked at his watch and saw it was four o'clock. Sweet Mary! he thought, with renewed irritation, hadn't Salas ever heard of the siesta?

'Alvarez?' said a sharp voice.

'Speaking, señor.'

'Where is the report on smuggling I asked you to send me three weeks ago?'

Was it really three weeks ago? 'Señor, the moment I received your orders, I began my investigations. But as you will readily understand, it is not a matter which can be quickly dealt with … '

'Why not?'

'Well … señor, smuggling is like a second job to some people — kind of runs in the family. They did it when the Moors were here, probably even as far back as the Romans … '

'I am not concerned with what happened in prehistoric times. I wish to know who is smuggling American cigarettes into this island now. They're being sold in bars all over the place and Chief Inspector Tamidir reports that the evidence quite definitely points to their entering at your end of the island … What have you done about the matter?'

'Everything possible, señor. But as you'll appreciate, when one is dealing with people who regard smuggling as a justifiable practice which their ancestors have carried on for generations …'

'Why do you insist on harping on the past?'

'Only to explain why all the usual channels of information dry up when it is a question of investigating smuggling, señor. No one is eager … '

'It is your job to make them eager. I want to know where these American cigarettes are being landed and who's landing them. And I want the information on my desk within the next week. Is that clear?' Superior Chief Salas cut the connection.

Alvarez replaced the receiver. Salas had, unfortunately, been born in Madrid — it explained a lot, without excusing it.

He yawned, looked at his watch again in near disbelief, then slowly stood up. He was a squat, broad-shouldered man and he experienced great difficulty in buying clothes which fitted him. His shirt, even when unbuttoned at the neck, was tight across his chest: had he worn a tie, as regulations demanded, he would, in the July heat, have been exceedingly uncomfortable.

He left his office and went downstairs. Outside the captain's office was a guard who, as soon as he saw Alvarez, looked at his watch, simulated total astonishment, and said: 'My God, it's not five yet! Where's the riot?'

Alvarez walked past him and out into the street. In the past, youngsters had shown respect towards their elders: now, they mocked them. Roll on the day when he retired and bought himself a small finca, sat out in the shade, and picked up handfuls of earth to let them slowly trickle through his fingers — and the nearest youngster was kilometres away.

He went up the road on the shady side and into the square. Since the land sloped, part was raised to provide a level surface and here chairs and tables were set out in front of two cafés. A number of people sat at the tables and he identified them from their reddened complexions as holidaymakers. The fools! he thought. They could be back at their hotels, sleeping.

He entered the Club Llueso, a square, attractive building to the south-east of the square and just beyond the steps down from the raised section. The bar was empty apart from the barman, who sat on a high stool and studied a football pool entry form.

Alvarez went over to the bar. 'Let's have a very large cognac.'

'You're early,' said the barman.

'Early for what?'

'It's like that, is it? It's the heat. The moment the thermometer tops thirty, people get gritty. I see it every year.' He poured out a large brandy and pushed the glass across the bar. 'Get outside of that and you'll find life's a bit more rosy.' He brought out a pack of Lucky Strike from under the bar, tore off one corner of the top paper, and tapped out a cigarette. 'And have a coffin-stick to go with it.'

'Thanks.' Alvarez flicked alight a lighter and lit the barman's cigarette, then his own. He inhaled a lungful of smoke and let it trickle slowly out of his nostrils, then drank. He replaced the glass on the bar and said: 'I've had the big white chief from Palma shouting at me over the telephone.'

'So that's what's got you even more mournful than usual!'

'He's giving himself blood pressure over smuggling.'

'Smuggling?' said the barman, very casually.

'American cigarettes. Says they're pouring ashore in their millions this end of the island … D'you think they could be?'

'How would I know? Palma's always on about this end of the island: blames it for everything. It's jealousy, that's what it is, because we've kept it beautiful and … '

'I wonder if there really is much smuggling these days?'

'Haven't I just told you, I don't know a bloody thing about it? But what I do say is this — suppose there is some smuggling, so what? A few fags nipped ashore when no one's looking — what harm's that doing Palma?'

'Well, smuggling's illegal.'

'So are most things. And anyway, people have been smuggling longer than the history books go back.'

'That's roughly what I told my superior chief.'

'So what did he say to that?'

'He hates history.' Alvarez finished the brandy and pushed the glass across. The barman refilled it.

'So you don't know anything?' asked Alvarez, as he picked up the refilled glass.

'I do my job, keep my nose clean, and my ears and eyes tight shut.'

'But possibly not your hands?' Alvarez stared at his cigarette and turned it round so that he could read the brand name.

The barman spoke angrily. 'The way the world is now, it doesn't pay to be kind and generous.'

'I know. It's a bitch.' Alvarez sighed. 'Ever heard of an Englishman being mixed up in the smuggling?'

'Didn't you hear me say I don't know nothing about anything?'

'Ah, well, that's the best way to keep out of trouble.' He finished the brandy. 'You know, you're right. I feel more cheerful now.'

'You're dead lucky, then,' replied the barman morosely.

*

Most of the time, Jim Meegan could regard himself with ironic detachment and his writing with the amused tolerance of someone who had learned to live with a slight disability: it was only when his jealousy over Helen grew out of hand, fed by too vivid an imagination, that he began to feel angrily sorry for himself.

He stared at the page in the typewriter and reread the nine lines of type. They weren't going to gain him immortality. Yet those nine lines represented two hours of work, two hours during which he had had to drag each word out, screaming, from the depths of his mind … The lion opened his mouth to roar and a mouse squeaked … He began each book with visions of a masterpiece and ended up by producing only popular entertainment (if that wasn't a gross misuse of the word 'popular'). He pulled out the paper, scrumpled it up, and threw it at the wastepaper basket. It missed and fell on the floor. Someone had once said that the wastepaper basket was a writer's best friend: he hadn't added that it might end up as his only friend.

He worked a new sheet of paper around the roller and typed 72 at the head of the page. Roughly 178 pages to go. Or 278 if this *was* to be the masterpiece: masterpieces mustn't be of a commercial length or the critics became doubtful and suspicious.

He was not wearing a shirt and the back of the chair was covered with a towel, but even so he sweated heavily. A drop of sweat trickled down from his neck. He watched it as soon as it came within his vision; apparently heading for the hairs on his chest, it suddenly and unaccountably swerved aside to slither down past his left nipple to his stomach. The sweat of Tolstoy and Dickens had probably run straight and true.

Page 72. Seventy-one pages completed, the hero and heroine about to go to bed together for the first time and he couldn't damn well get them moving. Perhaps they needed help from Masters and Johnson.

He heard a car and thought it was coming down the spur road, but then it continued on along the middle road of the urbanizacion. He'd expected Helen to be back a long time ago, but if she were with John Calvin then there was reason enough for her continuing absence. He heard the front door bang and thought she had, after all, arrived, but immediately afterwards he realized that Antonia, their part-time maid, had just left.

Calvin. What a hell of an inappropriate name for a man who was reputed to have had an affair with at least half the English married women in the area. Helen had laughed a lot with Calvin at the McKelties' cocktail party. True, at the McKelties one either had to laugh or drink like a fish, or both, if one were to survive, but there had been something about her laughter …

He trusted her. Implicitly. No set of circumstances, however compromising, could ever shatter his trust … Was she having an affair with John Calvin?

When she wasn't with him, he had the most intelligent and logical 'conversations' with her concerning their present relationship. They discussed his jealous fears, reviewed the reasons for these, she admitted to part of the blame and promised there would never again be cause for his doubts and jealousy, and in an adult manner they coped with an adult situation … But when she was actually with him … Jealousy seemed to strip him of all logic and reason.

Would it do any good if they left Mallorca? There must be other places where her bronchitis and asthma would respond as dramatically to climate as they had on the island — ironically, since so many Mallorquins suffered from both. If they left, they'd be leaving Calvin behind. But wouldn't there always be a Calvin wherever they went, until he and Helen had sorted themselves out?

He heard another car approach and this time it turned into the spur road which ended in a wide turning circle. A squeak, high in pitch and caused by the brakes, told him this was Helen. Play it cool, he told himself: cool and adult.

She entered the house by the front door, stepped past the kitchen into the sitting-room, and then came along the passage to the bedroom he used as an office. She was wearing a multi-coloured frock which suited her slightly angular shape and he remembered, with a sudden, painful shaft of memory, that the day he had first seen her she had been wearing a frock very similar in colour and design.

'How's it going, Jim? Is the inspiration flowing?'

She had spoken quickly, a shade nervously, he thought.

'Bloody awfully.' He pushed the low typing table away from himself.

She sat down on the unmade-up bed: she had an oval face filled with character and her mouth was curved as if forever about to break into a smile. She regarded him levelly. 'What's the matter that the work's not going too well?'

It was strange how, when questions concerning their relationship were put to him directly, he could seldom answer them directly. 'I keep thinking.'

She ran her tongue along her full lips, a frequent mannerism of hers when bothered, and reached up with her right hand to fidget with the top button of her dress. 'Couldn't you try thinking a little less?'

At their initial meeting, the first thing he had noticed about her had been her eyes. Deep blue, very direct, and obviously quick to suggest emotion. He answered her, trying to speak lightly. 'I can't cut back too far on thinking — apart from anything else, my job depends on it.'

'Why do you always … You knew what I meant, Jim. Why don't you try to think a little less intently about emotional matters?'

Why? Because … His emotions had always been too intense. (Weren't all artists intense by nature? There must be some obvious point of difference between them and the nine-to-five man on the Clapham omnibus.) 'I just can't change. If I get twisted into knots … ' His sense of humour belatedly came to his rescue. 'God! I sound like some self-tortured Dostoyevsky character.'

'Hardly.' She smiled back at him. 'You're not nearly loquacious enough. You'll need to learn to make a hundred words do the work of ten.'

'I wish I could. It would make a plot go much further.' She moved until she could rest her back against the wall. She began to fidget once more with the top button of her dress. 'Jim, the car was hell to start after lunch. I thought I'd never get it to go.'

'So what happened?' he asked, aware that his voice had become sharp. Where had she had lunch?

'I was just about to give up and call the garage when it finally spluttered into life. The poor old thing really is worn out. Don't you think it would be sensible to buy a new one?'

It would have to be her money which bought it and he had laid it down, when they married, that he paid for the essentials and her money was spent by her on whatever luxuries she wanted. That had been before successive governments, right and left, had knocked the pound into the gutter and inflation had all but crippled publishing. Now, she had to help pay for the essentials. That fact was resented by him even as he knew his resentment was childish and illogical.

'We could afford a Seat one two seven. Madge says hers is a jolly good car and she's had hardly any trouble with it apart from all that nonsense with the firm who supplied it.'

'There's no need. The garage will patch the old jalopy up,' he said, with a certainty he didn't feel.

She sighed, but did not press the matter. She thought his attitude towards her money was stupid, but she was perceptive enough to know that he saw things in the light of emotional pride and not logic.

'I'm packing in work for today.' He stood up and stretched. 'The masterpiece will have to wait.' He looked out at the sun-drenched, boulder-strewn land which was their garden and wondered again where she had had lunch and with whom. If he asked her, she would tell him. But he was scared of her answer.

CHAPTER II

The Hotel Azul, in Playa Nueva, was readily distinguishable from all the other slab-sided hotels around it because it was painted from top to bottom in a piercing shade of blue. It was U-shaped, had three bars, two dining-rooms, a TV lounge, a children's play area, and an outside swimming pool. Because the government had raised wages but the tour operators had fought any reasonable increase in prices, the management had cut the staff by a third: the remaining members were overworked and surly and the quality and quantity of the food had deteriorated sharply. Since ninety-eight per cent of the trade was with the package tour industry, any complaints were received with bored indifference.

Thomas Breeden stood in front of the reception desk in the foyer and impatiently watched the clerk trying to make out his bill, annoyed anyone could experience such difficulty in adding up a few figures. In the end the clerk passed the bill over and he checked it. He was not in the least surprised to discover an error of three pesetas. He pointed this out to the clerk, who was resentfully insolent that anyone should worry over so small a sum. However, when there had been farthings back in England, Breeden had worried over them. Watch the farthings and the halfpennies grew. Naturally, he was perfectly at home with the mechanics of decimal coinage, but had never really reconciled himself to it.

He took his wallet from his inside coat pocket. Even the clerks and waiters were no longer wearing coats because the heat was so great, but he believed in maintaining standards, especially in foreign countries where the natives were lax in such matters. He counted out three one thousand peseta notes and handed them over. The clerk gave him the wrong change and when this was pointed out, added an extra twenty-four pesetas with as much ill-will as possible. Breeden, carefully separating the twenty-five from the five and one peseta pieces, put the coins in his purse. He picked up his briefcase and suitcase, politely said goodbye to the clerk to show there was no lasting resentment, and walked towards the main doors.

A colleague at work had once been asked to describe Breeden. He'd thought for a while, scratched his head, and then confessed that he didn't really know what to say because Breeden was the most forgettable character he'd ever met. It was a harsh, but not wholly inaccurate, description. Breeden was of slightly above average height, well built but not fat, and his round face was so regularly proportioned that no single feature predominated, although his lips did lie a little straight and were rather thin: his hair was an unremarkable brown and his brown eyes seldom registered any emotion greater than pained surprise. He was a precise, pedantic man, but he saw precision and pedantry as virtues in a world where standards had plummeted and chaos had become the new religion.

He stepped out into the sunshine and within seconds began to sweat, but it did not occur to him to remove either his coat or his tie.

He walked down the steps and towards his hired car, parked under a pine tree.

'Hey! Hang on, old man ... Breeden, hang on there.'

He stopped and turned and stared at Willis, who was puffing along the pavement. His immediate thought was that it was a pity an Englishman should so lose his self-respect as to wear a crumpled shirt outside creased trousers and a pair of very battered flip-flops on his feet. Further, a moustache the size of Willis's was pure affectation.

Willis came up to where he stood. 'How the hell you can go around dressed up like this was St James's in November beats me.'

Those red-veined cheeks, thought Breeden, spoke of a long-standing devotion to alcohol.

'It's like a bloody oven today. As I said to the lady wife, it's going to be a real scorcher.'

'Did you wish to speak to me?' asked Breeden, happily unaware of the fatuousness of his question.

Willis took a large yellow handkerchief from his pocket and mopped some of the sweat from his forehead and neck. 'It's like this, old man. When I woke up, the lady wife went for me all ends up and said I'd been a right royal, stupid bastard.'

Breeden tried not to show his dislike of swearing, especially unnecessary swearing.

'She said I was so rude to you she was embarrassed.'

Remembering the horsy, gravel-voiced woman, Breeden decided it was unlikely anything had ever embarrassed her.

'She said I must apologize to you and, by Jove! she was dead right. I'm very sorry, old man, but I do tend to get a little enthusiastic at times. Especially when a tikkins-wallah comes … ' He stopped abruptly.

A taxi came up to the pavement and stopped and two passengers climbed out. Breeden took one pace towards his car.

'You can't rush off, old man.'

'I'm afraid I'm in a bit of a hurry, Mr Willis, and … '

'But I've got to apologize.'

'You have.'

'Without a liquid chotahazri to wash away the memories? Never. Rather my right arm dropped off. About turn and into the hotel bar, even if the bloody thieves do charge twice as much as Café Juma down the road.'

Breeden looked at his watch. 'It's only half past ten.'

'A bit late for the first one, I know, but we'll make up for it!' Willis laughed with explosive good humour as he made a grab for Breeden's suitcase and wrested it out of his hand, nearly knocking him to the ground. Willis hurried along to the steps and climbed them.

'I really haven't the time …' Breeden became silent as Willis reached the top of the steps and hurried to the doorway.

The main bar was to the right of the foyer. A group of newly arrived guests were milling round near the entrance, as they waited for the promised champagne cocktails, but the far half of the room was empty. Willis chose a table by one of the windows. 'What'll it be, then? One of the Willis specials? A Boomslinger — that's brandy with palo. Guaranteed to make the hairs grow.'

'Tomato juice, thank you.'

'What? God's grief, old man, you ought to have more respect for your liver. What about a Scorpion — rum and amontillado?'

'I really only want a tomato juice, thank you.'

Willis looked at him with ill-concealed scorn and then crossed to the bar. He returned with two glasses, one of which he passed across with distaste. 'My old quack had the right idea. "Keep the kidneys flushed out," he used to say, "and you'll never hear the stones clinking."' He raised his glass. 'Here's to the next one, old man. Now as I was saying, my lady wife says I owe you a real apology. Told me I was bloody rude. No argument. Plain bloody rude. But you didn't take offence, did you? It never worried me to be called a stupid bastard — that's the way you speak to your friends, after all. Still, I suppose I could've been a little less … Trouble is, when I meet a tikkins-wallah … ' He stopped.

'I'm not quite certain what you mean?'

'Just an expression, old man, means nothing. The fact is, I got just a little hot under the collar when you told me you were in the overseas investigation department of the Bank of England and had come out to the island to check on people who'd brought a few pennies out of England without paying the bloody premium. What I say is this. Suppose people do do that? So what? It's their money they've brought out, no one else's. Who in the hell has the right to stop 'em?'

'The Bank of England.'

'I was talking about a moral right. Not some goddamn iniquitous Gestapo law …'

'The Exchange Act, nineteen forty-seven. Under section … '

'Stuff the section!' Willis twirled each end of his moustache with thumb and forefinger, then lifted up his glass and drank it dry. 'Clauses, sections, acts, statutes … They give me gas. Stuff 'em, that's what I say.'

'Unfortunately, it seems that rather a lot of people on this island are of a similar persuasion.'

'Good. Why shouldn't they be?'

'The law is very clear, Mr Willis. Each family unit is allowed — if the senior member is under sixty-five years of age — to bring out of the country five thousand pounds free of dollar premium. Any sum beyond that amount must be applied for through the Bank of England … '

'Red tape. Bureaucracy gone mad, jobs for the bloody boys. If I had my way, there'd be gallows lining the roads from Downing Street to the Houses of Parliament … Drink up. It's time for the next one.'

'I never have more than one, thank you.'

'You'll have to watch it, or you'll end up dehydrated, like a bloody prune, what?' Willis stood up, picked up his glass, and crossed to the bar. He ordered two large brandies and when he was served emptied one glass into the other and carried the full glass back to the table. He produced a pack of Chesterfields. 'Have a gasper?'

'Thank you, but I do not smoke.'

'No smoking, no drinking? What's your hobby? Little girls?'

Breeden was shocked.

'I want you to understand, old man, no offence intended last night. It's just that I got a bit excited at one stage. But when a bloke starts talking about some goddamn stupid law just because of something happening ...'

'I feel I must make the position quite clear. Under sub-section G of section forty, Mr Willis, as amended under the 'fifty-nine act which amended the 'fifty-one amended act, any person found guilty of illegally exporting sterling beyond the United Kingdom (within this context, of course, United Kingdom means for the sake of convenience the United Kingdom, the Isle of Man, and the Channel Islands) may be fined up to three times the sum of the premium avoided. And under sub-section six of section fifty-three, as amended under the 'sixty-two act, any assets remaining in the United Kingdom may be called upon to meet the sum due. Assets, under sub-section eight of the same section, include a life interest in a trust.'

'It's immoral.'

'It is the law.'

Willis finished his brandy. 'Stuff the law.'

'Proof of illegal export of sterling can often be obtained by reference to documents signed by the person concerned and submitted by him to the Bank of England. It is an unfortunate fact that experience has taught us that hitherto honest persons are prepared to perjure themselves in order to avoid paying the premium ... '

'Thank God there are some free men left.'

'... One of the more common forms of perjury, regrettably carried out with the aid of foreign solicitors, is to declare the value of the house bought as very much less than, in fact, it is, thereby obscuring the illegal exportation of sterling.'

'Shows initiative.'

'However, as has been said, "To those who would suppress it, truth may verily become a hydra."'

'What are you getting at now, for God's sake?'

'The mythological water-monster, Mr Willis, whose many heads grew again whenever they were cut off.'

'What's that to do with buying a house? If you tikkins-wallahs could only speak English instead of choking yourselves on sections and sub-sections and water-monsters, it'd be a hell of a lot easier for us.'

Breeden's briefcase was on his lap. He began to tap on it with the fingers of his right hand. 'If I remember correctly, Mr Willis, when your application for permission to buy a house on this island reached us, the purchase price was given as one million two hundred and fifty thousand pesetas.'

Willis finished his drink.

'You bought it just over eighteen months ago and paid the premium on the difference between five thousand pounds and ten thousand three hundred pounds which was the value of a million and a quarter pesetas at one hundred and twenty point three … '

'So I paid the premium.'

'Mr Willis, I am not an estate agent and so have no specialized knowledge of house values, but having seen much of your very nice home — you may remember that for a time last night I became a trifle apprehensive for my own safety and entered several of the rooms in a hurry — I should imagine that the property cost you considerably more than a million and a quarter pesetas.'

'You were bloody snooping.'

'I wonder if ten million pesetas would be a more accurate reflection of the purchase price?'

Willis became very red in the face.

'The difference between the true value and the declared value of your house, with a rate of sixty-two per cent actually payable, would possibly attract a premium of fifty-four thousand seven hundred and five pounds. If the maximum fine were levied, you would owe one hundred and thirty-four thousand one hundred and sixteen pounds. A sum which, I fear, would consume all the capital you presently hold invested in Government stock, together with the large proportion of your life interest, commuted (under sub-section thirteen), in the trust set up under the will of your late aunt.'

Willis stared with shocked horror at Breeden, unable to comprehend such passionless malignancy, then went over to the bar and ordered another two brandies. He drank them before returning to the table.

Breeden cleared his throat and for the first time was less than certain in manner. 'Mr Willis, I should like at this stage of our discussion to … Perhaps I can best put the matter in this way. We of the overseas investigation branch are ready, when circumstances warrant, to take a pragmatic attitude. Do you understand what I mean?'

'No.'

'There are times in any job when the results may become more important than the means used to attain them. Do you now follow me?'

'No.'

Breeden began to tap his fingers more rapidly on the briefcase. 'Information given by a person who has contravened the regulations may, in certain circumstances — for instance, when he has helped us uncover the means by which the money has been illegally exported — lead to his offence being viewed in a more lenient light than would otherwise be the case.'

Willis looked up and his face was flushed. 'Are you trying to say that if I tell you what I know, you'll go easy on any fine?'

'We make no promises, but we do ... '

'Stuff your promises. You're just a creeping tikkins-wallah.'

Breeden suffered no angry resentment. Indeed, if anything, he almost welcomed such abuse since it enabled him to be magnanimous. 'Naturally, the decision is peculiar to each individual and his case.'

'You can take a running jump.'

Breeden coughed. 'I admire your courage, if not your wisdom. Your style of living is plainly high and it takes courage to undertake a course of action in the name of principle which must lead to a sharp diminution of that style.'

There was a long silence. 'What exactly do you want?' Willis finally demanded hoarsely.

'The details of how you were able to move the money from England to here.'

'I ... If I tell you what happened, I'm not going to name names.'

'I am afraid names are rather important.'

'I'm not giving any, no matter what. I'm no informer.'

Breeden nodded, as if sympathetic towards such sentiments. 'Perhaps it will not be strictly necessary — we in the overseas investigation branch are neither as blind nor as deaf as people would like to believe. I will mention names — you can acknowledge whether they hold any special significance for you. By no stretch of the imagination can that be considered informing on your part.'

Willis picked up his glass and went over to the bar.

It was interesting, Breeden reflected with a sense of moral superiority, how most men's sense of honour was proportionally related to their financial status. He undid the two straps of the briefcase, opened it, and brought out a sheet of paper. The first name on the short list of names was that of John Calvin.

CHAPTER III

Brenda Calvin was, to use her own words, Avrilesque — she meant Junoesque. She often jokingly said that Raphael would have been glad to have her as a model — she meant Rubens. Being full of bubbling good humour, and ever ready to laugh at herself, she didn't give a damn if her bodily measurements were no longer what they had been a few years before.

She moved in the bed until she could reach across to the chair and bring out of her handbag a cheque-book. 'What's up?' asked Steven Adamson.

'I wondered if I'd any money left in the bank.'

'What a hell of a time to worry about that.'

'I always worry about something afterwards: I had a pet of a psychiatrist once who told me that it's because of my fear of pregnancy. But since I don't dare think in terms of pregnancy, in case that should start something, I worry about something else.'

'Surely to God you're taking the pill?'

'Of course I am. When I can remember to.' She sat upright and opened the cheque-book. She had curly blonde hair, a round, cheerful face with welcoming brown eyes, a nose which almost turned up, and very full lips. Her skin was beautifully tanned, including her breasts and hips since she sun-bathed nude on the flat roof of her flat, despite the fact that this was overlooked by the end rooms on the two upper floors of the nearby hotel. 'Hell's teeth!' she exclaimed.

'Now what's the matter?'

'They're bound to be wrong, aren't they? The banks always get things wrong. According to what they told me the other day, I'm now down to my last two thousand pesetas.' She stared at the cheque-book, then shrugged her smooth, well filled shoulders. 'What the hell! The bank will bounce the cheques if there isn't enough in the account to meet 'em.'

He propped himself up on one elbow. 'You know something? You're immoral.' He was younger than she. He was handsome, in a hard, self-confident manner. Yet there was something about his mouth which hinted at a weakness.

She replaced the cheque-book in her handbag, then lay back. After a while she said: 'I'm not really.'

'Not really what?'

'Immoral. It's just that things happen when I'm not ready for them. Like seeing that red coat and wanting it so badly.'

'You could've worked out you couldn't afford it.'

'Then someone else would have bought it. Don't be such a spoilsport.'

'At least you'd have had some money left in the bank.'

'It never seems to stay in the bank, whether I see a red coat or not. John was always going on and on at me for spending, but as I said to him, I can't help it. Some people are born like that. It used to get him so furious because he's really a miser.'

He folded his arms above and behind him so that he could rest his head in the palms. 'Have you seen him recently?'

'The other day, when I asked him for some money.' She laughed. 'That hurt and he started trying to tell me how poor he'd become. I told him, pack up spending money on other people's wives.'

'How did he react to that?'

'Got quite shirty for some reason and told me to stop looking for motes. When I got back here I looked the word up and found out what he was getting at. I think.'

'You reckon he knows about us?'

'God's grief, of course he does! And so does everyone else. You can't sneeze once in this place without everyone else knowing you've got a cold. By the way, did you know Daphne's having a bomb with Basil?'

He ignored the question. 'What was his attitude?'

'Basil's?'

'Can't you ever stick to one subject?'

'Not if it's a boring one.' She stood up and walked across to the window.

When she opened the shutters, he said angrily: 'Come away from there, you've nothing on.'

'No one can see me and even if they can, what the hell? I look just like everyone else. Why do men always rush to look at women in the nude anyway? They know exactly what they're going to see.' She stared out through the open window. Beyond the road, which was often very busy during the season, was a short stretch of sand and then the sea. Today the sea had three different shades of blue, the darkest where the bottom was covered with a heavy growth of seaweed: she often studied the patterns of colour and tried to conjure pictures out of them. Beyond the western pier of the harbour, to her left, a sailing boat had just hoisted a red and white spinnaker which was now billowing because it was not correctly set, and the moving colours excited her. 'Steve, come here and look. It's so pretty.'

'What is?'

'A boat with an enormous red and white striped sail.'

'That's probably Alan. Doesn't know the bows from the stern — talk about a bloody waste, having a yacht like that.'

As she watched, the spinnaker suddenly collapsed and trailed in the water. 'It's dead now and it's all your fault.'

He climbed off the bed and crossed the room to stand behind her. He put his hands round her and cupped her flesh. 'What's dead?'

'The sail.'

He looked out through the window. 'I told you so — that is Alan's yacht. Instead of a beautiful job like that, he ought to have a dinghy.'

She leaned her head back until she could nuzzle his cheek. 'So why are you such a dog-in-the-manger? You can't stand anyone having something you haven't, can you?'

'I hate seeing anything as beautiful as that yacht being completely wasted,' he answered sharply.

'You ought to be like me. I don't care what anyone does or has.'

'Sure. Just a simple little girl at heart.' He stared moodily at the yacht, whose crew were just beginning to clear the spinnaker from the water. 'That yacht should be owned by a proper yachtsman, not a fair-weather lollipop — she's an ocean racer.'

'You say that with a hell of a lot more feeling than you ever say anything to me.'

'Ships are faithful.'

'God, it's hot!' she said, breaking away from him. 'And you feel like a furnace. Let's go for a swim.'

He returned to the bed and sat down on it. 'How did he take the news?'

'How did Frederick take what news?'

He looked up and spoke in an exasperated tone. 'Half an hour with you and my mind's looping the loop. Where the hell did Frederick come from? … How did your husband react to knowing about you and me, apart from shouting about motes?'

She shrugged her shoulders and her well filled breasts bobbed up and down invitingly. 'I never did know what he was thinking. He's one of those awful men who never loses his temper and can smile all the time. The only thing which blows his cool is money: he'll have a throm if he thinks he might lose a hundred pesetas.'

'Then how did he react when you asked him for money?'

She laughed as she looked at him. 'Worried I won't get any?'

'That's a bloody thing to say.'

She walked over to the bed and cuddled him against her body. 'Didn't I ever tell you, I never know what my tongue's going to say?'

He began to stroke her flanks. 'Why on earth did you ever let him have your money in the first case?'

She looked faintly puzzled. 'Why not? I've never understood the stuff and he said he knew all about it and would invest it so that it would make me a fortune.'

'Make him a fortune, you mean. He's swiped the lot and pays you out as little as he reckons he can get away with.'

'He swears it's all safely invested.'

'You've got to be joking. Or else you're even more naive than I thought.'

She stepped away from him and picked up a pack of cigarettes from the bedside table. She lit a cigarette with a small, slim gold lighter. 'You don't begin to understand John. You're just like Dick.'

'I'm nothing like Dick,' he said, with sudden annoyance. 'If I thought I were really anything like him, I'd cut my throat.'

'It's funny you can't stand him. I think he's a duck.'

'He sure quacks a lot.'

She giggled. 'As a matter of fact he doesn't like you very much. Do you know what he calls you?'

'No.'

'I don't think I'd better tell you.'

'Don't.'

'If you're going to be like that! … Master World.'

'I'll smash his head in next time I see him.'

'But where's your sense of humour? He's such fun. He knows all the best scandal and when I'm bored I go and have tea with him.'

'You're not to see him again.'

'Don't be so pugnacious.'

'I'm telling you, cut him out.'

She spoke laughingly, yet there was a note in her voice which wasn't usually there. 'Steve, love, I'm nearly as old as my bust measurements, so I'll decide who I see and who I don't. Don't start getting like him.'

'Me get like Dick. I've just told you … '

'Francis.'

'Who the hell's talking about Francis?'

'I am.' She stubbed out her cigarette. 'Come on, let's put our costumes on and have a swim. Last one in the sea is a cissy.'

*

Whenever he was introduced to someone he had not previously met, Percival Goldstein said: 'I am not a Jew. My father's family three generations back was Dutch.' He was a man of middle height, with a large head that was almost bald: in artificial light it shone as if he had covered it with oil. His eyes were very dark brown, almost black, and behind his thick-lensed glasses they were forever on the move, as if he could look at nothing for very long.

He and his wife, Amanda, lived in a large and well built house — it was one of the very few buildings which didn't leak whenever it rained hard — on the side of a small hill on the road to Cala Roig. She was fifteen years younger than he and looked twenty years younger. She was almost the same height and so wore flat-soled shoes in order not to look taller. She had tight curly hair — her nickname to his sharp annoyance was Bubbles — azure blue eyes set slightly wide apart, an attractive face which was slightly spoiled by a suggestion of uncertainty, and a slim body which belied her age of forty.

Goldstein stood in front of the grey steel filing cabinet, at the far end of the very large sitting-room, and searched through the papers in the top drawer. He said, in his dry, flat-toned voice: 'I can't find the receipt for groceries bought in the second week in March.'

She looked up from the copy of *Woman's Own* which she had bought earlier in the Port. 'Can't you, dear?'

'Did you get one?'

'I can't really remember. It's rather a long time ago.'

'How can I work out the household figures if I haven't the receipts?'

'Why not just call it five hundred pesetas?'

He looked at her with annoyed surprise, then resumed his search.

After a while, she said: 'There's a simply lovely three-quarter-length coat advertised this week. D'you think we could ask Martha to get one in my size and bring it out next month?'

'I thought you had a large number of coats already?'

'Love, a woman needs a new coat from time to time, to cheer her up.'

'Why are you feeling depressed?'

'I don't mean it exactly like that. Not literally. But you know how a woman is … '

'We can't afford it,' he said definitely. He slammed the cabinet drawer shut and there was the sharp and ugly noise of clashing metal.

'But it only costs fifteen quid … '

'I've asked you before not to use that ugly word.'

'Fifteen pounds, then.'

'Amanda, until I am able to work out the figures for last year, I have no way of knowing how our finances stand.'

'You must have. What is it? You want to get your own back on me because I forgot to get some stupid little receipt?'

He looked at her over the tops of his spectacles. 'I am not small-minded.'

'I'm sorry, love, I shouldn't have said that … But you do get so upset just because I forget things. You know I've never had a very good memory. And anyway, most of the shops out here don't really know what a receipt is.'

'That is absurd. They are, by law, bound to issue one. What you mean is, they're too lazy to give you one and you haven't the business sense to demand one.' He crossed over to the nearer armchair and sat down. He stared out through an opened window at the mountains, light grey in the sharp sunshine, with an occasional patch of green to show where a lone pine tree struggled to survive, and complacently thought that the view added at least a million pesetas to the value of the house.

She looked again at the coloured illustration of the coat. It wasn't very stylish and at that price couldn't be of very good material, but it would have been colourful and gay and her life was short of colour and gaiety.

'By the way,' he said, 'the Drays are coming to supper.'

'Oh, my God!'

'Now what's the matter?'

'First you've only just told me and I can't think what I can give them to eat; second, they're the most boring old couple on the island.'

'I don't like to hear you talk like that.'

'Why can't we have someone under sixty for a change? The Jacksons. They're such fun … '

'She is not a very pleasant person.'

'You only dislike her because she teased you at that party.'

He spoke with great dignity. 'I consider that she was unpardonably rude.'

'She'd had a drink or two, but she was good fun and was making everyone laugh. Isn't it better to make people laugh than be like the Drays who tell you all about their colds before the meal, their tummy upsets during it, and their geriatric pains with the coffee?'

'They are a couple of very intelligent persons who have the misfortune to suffer considerable ill health.'

'What you mean is, they're stinking rich.'

'Sometimes, Amanda, I wonder if you ever have a serious, worthwhile thought in your head.'

'That shouldn't disturb you. You didn't marry me for my brains.'

'That was quite unnecessary.' He looked at his wristwatch.

'It's time for tea, I think.'

She left the room. The kitchen was tiled in old Mallorquin tiles, rich of colour, which depicted various costumes traditionally associated with certain jobs — they had been expensive. The kitchen equipment was very extensive. Her husband never minded spending money when it was obvious that he had done so.

She switched on the electric kettle and put the tin of Lapsang Souchong tea near the teapot: from the very large refrigerator she brought out the plate on which were four pastries. From the day they had been married, he had had Lapsang tea and three different pastries at five o'clock every afternoon. She wondered whether his first wife had catered quite so thoroughly to his precise, finicky ways. Probably not. His first wife had been his own age and wealthy in her own right. Perhaps he had had to do everything for her to make certain of inheriting her money and now he was gaining his revenge.

The kettle boiled and she poured water into the teapot to warm it. Before their marriage, ten years ago, a villa in Mallorca had seemed to her the very height of luxurious happiness. Now, she knew that for her such a life was a slow form of death.

She emptied the teapot, put in three heaped spoonfuls of tea, and added water. She placed the teapot, silver milk jug, a single slice of lemon, pastries, silver sugar bowl, two silver teaspoons, two plates, and two cups and saucers, on the heavily engraved silver tray. Percival said that the crest in the centre of the tray was his family's. She preferred to believe he'd bought the tray and appropriated the crest: instant aristocratic ancestors.

She returned to the sitting-room, which was looking very beautiful since the sun had moved until sunshine flooded through the windows to pick out the colours of the two large Chinese carpets.

She put the tray down on the walnut piecrust table and poured him out his first of two cups of tea and put in the slice of lemon. She was convinced he would rather have milk and sugar, as she did, but Lady Eastmore had once told him that Lapsang tea should only be drunk with a slice of lemon. She pulled out the bottom table of a nest of four, and put that by the side of his chair: she placed cup and saucer on it. She proffered him the tray and he studied the pastries for a long time before he made up his mind and chose one.

She sat down and poured herself out a cup of tea and, with a brief, futile sense of defiance, added sugar and milk. She ate the slice of Swiss roll with lemon filling because she knew he didn't like it. She lit a cigarette.

'Aren't you smoking rather heavily these days?' he asked.

'Not really.'

'How many have you had today?'

'I've no idea.'

'You should have. I can't think why you continue to smoke when you know how dangerous the habit is.'

'I can imagine worse deaths than cancer of the lungs.'

'Such as?'

'Living too long.'

He spoke coldly. 'Just what is that supposed to mean?'

'That I don't want to live to be as old as the Drays.'

'No doubt your attitude would change if I suffered an early demise?'

'Don't, please, start that up again, Perce.'

'How many times have I asked you not to call me Perce?'

She forced herself to smile, to try to move away from an open row. 'That makes two thousand four hundred and sixteen.'

He was not amused.

'The trouble is, love, Percival is such a mouthful and Perce seems so much more friendly.'

'I have always disliked diminutives.' He put his cup and saucer down on the table. 'I think I would like some more tea — and, perhaps, another of those pastries.' He spoke as if there might have been some doubt.

She poured him out a second cup of tea and passed him a second pastry.

He ate slowly, chewing every mouthful very thoroughly. When he'd finished, she stood up and carried over the tray so that he could take the last pastry. Half-way through eating this, he paused and took a handkerchief from his pocket. He brushed his lips with it, then looked at her over the tops of his spectacles. 'I went into Palma this morning.' He resumed eating.

'I know. I saw you off.'

'I met the Phillpots on Jaime Three.'

She was upset, but did what she could to hide the fact. When she spoke, she fiddled with her cigarette, rolling it backwards and forwards between finger and thumb so that the smoke rose in wavy billows. 'I thought they'd gone back home?'

'They had to delay their flight … Stella told me you did not go to lunch there on Monday.' He stared fixedly at her.

She smoked.

'Well? Where did you go at lunch-time?'

'Nowhere special. I just drove around.' She looked quickly at him. 'I knew you wouldn't understand me if I told you just the truth.'

He took off his spectacles and cleaned them with a handkerchief, then replaced them.

She struggled to sound totally unworried. 'Every now and then I want to be on my own. But you can't seem to understand and you get all fussed if I want to go out, so I just said Stella had invited me to lunch to make everything easier.'

'You knew they were supposed to be going back to England. That's why you used their name. So I wouldn't be able to check up on what you told me.'

'Maybe. But only because I knew you wouldn't … '

'Where did you go?'

'I just drove about the place, to be on my own and with nothing definite to do. In this house, everything has to be done by the clock. Breakfast at eight-thirty, lunch at one, tea at five, dinner at nine. And if I'm ten minutes late, you're in the kitchen, demanding to know what's wrong. It's a wonderful treat to be somewhere that I don't need to give a damn whether it's one or three o'clock.'

'Who were you with?'

She stubbed out her cigarette. 'I was on my own and just driving round the roads …'

'You were with a man, weren't you?' His voice rose. 'I'm not a fool, so don't try and treat me as one. You were with a man. You arranged to meet him on Monday.'

'For God's sake, Perce … '

'Don't call me Perce.'

She lit another cigarette.

CHAPTER IV

Alvarez parked on the wrong side of the no-parking sign. He climbed out on to the pavement and stared at a lithesome, long-legged girl who was walking along the pavement — she was dressed in a minimum bikini and a floppy sun hat. He was sufficiently old-fashioned to regret that any young lady should appear on the roads in so scanty a dress, yet not so old that he failed to appreciate the sight if she did.

He followed the girl to the T-junction, where the Llueso, sea front, and Playa Nueva roads met, and there he carried on, across the road to the eastern arm of the harbour while she turned right.

Like most islanders, the sea and boats held a special meaning for him and he liked nothing better than to wander around a harbour, however small, staring at the boats and smelling the salt/fish/tar/paint smell which accompanied them. He was not a man who could clearly identify his own emotions, yet he knew that Puerto Llueso, ringed by mountains, the bay deep blue in the sun and occasionally so still that he almost hesitated to breathe out too deeply in case it destroyed the peace, offered him a sense of inner contentment that was beyond value. At such times he had consciously to take note of the kiosks selling hot dogs and ice creams to the tourists, and of the tourist buses and the large yachts owned by tourists, to retain a valid sense of grievance.

He walked up the cobbled eastern arm and came abreast of the fish restaurant. It was reputedly a very good restaurant, with prices to back up that reputation, and once it had been almost exclusively patronized by the English: now most of the patrons were French or German. When he thought of how the once mighty pound sterling had fallen down on its face, he was prepared to believe there was some natural justice in the world.

He walked on, past the ferries which took trippers to Parelona beach, past the Club Nautico where yachtsmen and would-be yachtsmen sat and drank, and reached the end of the arm. To his left was the harbour entrance and straight ahead was the curving western arm. Almost opposite there was tied up a two-masted schooner, surely seaworthy enough to cross any ocean? How much money did she cost just to keep tied up there? he wondered.

Enough to make most Mallorquin families whistle with envy — not that there were now many poor Mallorquins: tourism might have ruined parts of the island, but it had enriched most of the islanders.

With a throbbing roar of noise, an old flying-boat, rolling back the years, began to taxi across the water before taking off. Higher in key, and far more irritating in quality, was the noise from an approaching speedboat which was towing two water-skiers: as he watched, the skiers criss-crossed each other's wakes, the man ducking under the woman's line. For a short time, the intensely blue water was slashed by the white wakes of boat and skiers.

He turned away and strolled back along the arm until he came to the fishing boats. A single fisherman was mending a net, weaving his stubby shuttle in and out of the small mesh with bewildering speed. Alvarez stopped. 'How's life with you?'

The fisherman looked up, shielding his eyes from the sun with a hand that was calloused from years of work on boats. 'What's brought you down to the Port? Has somebody robbed one of the banks?'

'Quite possibly. But so far no one's woken up enough to discover the fact.' Alvarez hunkered down on his heels. 'How's the fishing going these days?'

'If it got any thinner, there wouldn't be any.'

'You know, old man, you're worse than any farmer with all your moans.'

'Spit in the eye of the Virgin if I'm lying when I tell you that it's a good day now if we catch a quarter of the fish we'd've caught when I was a nipper.'

'You'll get paid a lot more for what you do catch.'

'And what's it buy at a time when prices rise between merienda and supper?'

'Enough booze and baccy to have kept you out of your coffin.'

The fisherman chuckled. 'Aye, I can still empty a glass or two, even if I did spit out the last of me teeth the other day over a crust. And I can still do a day's work. Not like you. You've got fat, like a sow in litter. Too much sitting around.'

'I work much too hard,' agreed Alvarez. He took a pack of cigarettes from his pocket and offered it. 'I'm looking for Pedro. He's on the boats.'

'Pedro?' The fisherman struck a match.

When Alvarez leaned forward to light his cigarette from the match in the seamed, cupped hands, he gained an acrid smell of stale fish. 'That's right. Pedro,' he answered, as he leaned back.

'Take your pick.' The fisherman laughed shrilly. 'The boats are filled with Pedros.'

'He baits his hooks with more than squid and catches more than fish.'

'He's lucky, ain't he?'

'And full of initiative. He smuggles.'

'Smuggles? What are you on about? Who around here would smuggle?'

'Anyone who reckoned to get away with it.'

The fisherman hawked and spat. When he spoke, he seemed unaware of any contradiction with what he'd just said. 'There's nowt to a bit of smuggling. It's in a man's bones, like the salt water.'

'I know that, but my boss doesn't.'

'Then he's a silly bastard.'

'I'm not arguing.'

'A bloke brings a few cigarettes and watches ashore — in times of few fishes, he'd starve if he didn't.'

'My boss hasn't heard about the watches yet.'

'Then he's a silly deaf bastard,' said the fisherman and cackled with laughter until he choked and Alvarez had to lean forward to thump him on the back. 'It's me tubes. The quack said as I ought to be dead, they're in such a state.'

'You've a few years yet, by the look of you, before they plant you out.' Alvarez tapped his cigarette and the lazy breeze spilled the ash into the water. Several tourists strolled past, looking at them with open curiosity. Assimilating all the local colour they could, he thought. 'Where will I find the Pedro I want to talk to?'

'I don't know.'

'Old man, you're so old you know everything about everybody.'

The fisherman moved his knees, which caused the shuttle to tumble down the side of the net: he retrieved it. He drew on the cigarette, holding it into his palm as a seaman did in a gale to shield the burning end. He looked briefly at Alvarez, then beyond the nearest building at the bay. He waited, but Alvarez's calm, endless patience, bovine in its intensity, convinced him that the detective would wait for ever for an answer. He cleared his throat. 'There's Pedro the bull.'

'A strong bloke?'

'I've seen him lift as many baskets as two other blokes put together.'

'I'd better be polite to him, then. Where's he live?'

'Calle Bunyola.'

'What's the name or number of his house?'

'Never heard it.'

'OK — someone'll tell me.' Alvarez stood up. 'Keep working hard, old man. Maybe the fish'll come back in their millions and make your fortune.'

The fisherman shrugged his shoulders. 'It doesn't worry me no more.'

Alvarez left and walked to the road end of the harbour arm. He waited for the stream of traffic to pass, then crossed.

When he came abreast of a memento shop he stopped and stared at the medley of carved figures, egg-cups, egg-timers, nutcrackers, and corkscrews in wood, belts of wood and leather, pottery figures, glass animals, postcards … In the old days, he thought, there had been on the island a few men who created beauty in wood with skill and devotion so that their Virgin Marys had been women who suffered for all mankind: now, many men created with machines and their endless Don Quixotes were ugly works of commerce. The tourists destroyed even as their money built.

Calle Bunyola led off to the right of the Llueso road and was two hundred metres long. Beyond it was an urbanizacion in the early stages of development with a large number of empty plots where an earlier lush growth of weeds had been dried by the sun so that now the area looked a parched wasteland.

An elderly woman, dressed in widow's black, was sitting out on the pavement in the shade of her house. She directed him to the house with green shutters.

He opened the front door, stepped inside, and called out. As he waited he looked round the room, part hall, part sitting-room: it was spotlessly clean and in one corner was a large colour television set.

A man, very tall for a Mallorquin, with broad shoulders, a heavy beard, dark brown eyes that were noticeably lively, an unruly mop of black and very tight curly hair, came out of the room to the right.

'Good morning,' said Alvarez, in Mallorquin.

Collom stared at him, a slight frown on his piratical face. Then he nodded. 'You're the copper from Llueso?'

'Right for one.'

'Who likes cognac?'

'Right for two.'

'So how d'you like it?'

'In a large glass.'

Collom laughed, a deep, belly laugh, then returned into the room from which he'd come. He brought out two balloon glasses, half filled with brandy, and he passed one over. 'Here's damnation to all teetotallers.'

Alvarez drank, noting with pleasure that the brandy was a good one, and he went on drinking until all that remained in the glass was the small amount it was customary and polite to leave.

'You really do like cognac!' said Collom, a note of reluctant respect in his voice. His own glass still had some brandy in it and he drank this quickly. 'Let's have your glass. Life's too short to waste time.'

When he came back into the room with the glasses refilled, Alvarez took one of the glasses from him and then said: 'How d'you like colour telly?'

'It's great. Come and watch it sometime when you've nothing better to do.'

'I'll maybe take you up on that … You must be doing all right if you can afford to buy a colour set at over ninety thousand?'

Collom spoke carelessly. 'I took an old Kraut out fishing one day and he caught so many big fish he reckoned he'd had the finest day of his life. He was going back to Germany to live there and couldn't be bothered to take the set back with him so he gave it to me as a thank-you.'

'A real slice of luck.'

'I get lucky sometimes.'

'I don't,' said Alvarez lugubriously. 'I've a boss who comes from Madrid and can't grow a crop of ulcers fast enough. He makes sure I don't get lucky. He doesn't understand us islanders.'

'Spaniards!' said Collom contemptuously. 'They ought to ship the bloody lot of 'em back to the Peninsula.'

'He gets all excited over things that don't really matter. Like cigarettes being smuggled ashore.'

Collom fiddled with his beard. 'Silly bugger! There's been smuggling since anyone's ever lived here. What the hell's the use of living on an island if not to smuggle?'

'I tried to tell him that, but he wouldn't listen. All get up and go, that's him. Says that if the smuggling isn't stopped right away, he's going to send a detachment of Guards into the Port to search every house to see who's living it up rich.'

'That could be interesting.'

Alvarez finished his drink.

Collom said: 'Anyone who can drink like you'd make a bloody good fisherman.' He held out his hand for the other's glass.

When Alvarez was given his glass back, he held the bowl in the palm of his hand to warm it. 'As I've always said, a little bit of smuggling's good for the soul and the pocket.'

Collom, broad shoulders slightly hunched, stared at him, his eyes watchful and hard.

'But things get different when it's done on a big scale and that's when my boss hears about it and worries. And what worries my boss, worries me. There's another thing: when it gets real big, in come the foreigners.'

'Foreigners?' said Collom roughly. 'There's never been a foreigner out at night. The lads'd tip him into the sea and leave him for the crabs.'

'I don't mean actually out on the boats: where'd you find a foreigner with the guts to do that?'

'Then what?'

'Professional smuggling needs big money and if the foreigners haven't got anything else, they've got plenty of that. Someone's been putting up big money.'

'Yeah?'

'I want his name.'

'You won't find it here.'

Alvarez drank. He held his glass at the level of his mouth and looked at Collom over the rim. 'You know something? If my boss came in here and saw that colour telly set and tasted this cognac, he'd have you marched off to the clink so fast your throat wouldn't have time to dry out.'

'I don't know nothing.'

'Who's the banker? The Englishman called John Calvin?'

'Who the hell's he?' But Collom couldn't quite hide his expression of shocked surprise.

Alvarez finished his brandy.

CHAPTER V

Meegan stood in the garden — since he loathed gardening, it was a garden only in name — and stared up at the house being built four hundred metres away, on the rising slope of the mountain which backed the urbanizacion. Rumour had it that this house — an odd mixture of arches and roofs at different levels — was being built for a Frenchman. He could never understand why any Frenchman should want to build a holiday house on an urbanizacion on Mallorca when he could choose the South of France.

He turned and crossed to one of the deck-chairs on the small patio. Once he was sitting, he looked at his watch. Twenty minutes to drinking time. He sometimes mocked himself for adhering to a six o'clock 'sundown' since he was a person who detested routine, but he was certain that if ever he allowed himself a drink whenever he felt like it, without reference to the clock, he would soon become as alcoholically inclined as so many of the retired English who couldn't find enough to do to occupy their time.

He heard a rustle of sound from his left and looked out at the boulder-strewn area of rough grass, cistus, spurge, dwarf fan palms, thistles, stunted prickly-pear cactus, and single century plant, but for quite a time couldn't pick out what insect or animal had made the sound — then he saw an olive-brown praying mantis, reared up in its 'praying' position. Was the mantis one of the species of insects in which the female ate its mate after copulation?

Sometimes, when his mood was bitter as well as ironic, he'd tell himself that if only he'd been born with either less or more ability, he'd have been successful. Less and he couldn't have hoped to make a living from writing so he'd have tried something else, more and his books would have sold enough to provide him with a real living. But as things were, success at writing stayed out of reach, yet unfortunately not out of sight.

Lacking any alteration in his ability, a different mental attitude would have been helpful. Ask nine men out of ten what made for the perfect marriage and their answers would be, an attractive, passionate wife with money. Helen was very attractive, very passionate, and she had quite a

35

large private income. Yet only a fool or a blind optimist would call their marriage perfect.

Jealousy was one of the deadly sins. For his money, it was by far and away the most deadly. It crept up unidentified, even unseen, grabbed its victim with all the tenaciousness of a lamprey latching on to a stone, and then pumped out its poison day after day. But at first the victim didn't realize he was being poisoned.

Everything Helen said or did was, for him, ambiguously natured. If she was in a very cheerful mood, was it because she had recently been with Calvin or merely because she was happy? If she was depressed, was it because she couldn't visit Calvin, or merely because she was feeling sad? When in answer to his questioning she'd told him she'd met Calvin in the square and had had a couple of drinks with him at one of the outside tables — could anything be less compromising? — had she told him because that was the truth in full, or because she knew she'd been seen with Calvin and she was trying to disarm suspicion? Did she answer his questions because she always told him the truth, or because by doing so she could seem to be?

Calvin had a reputation Don Juan would not have scorned. Men couldn't understand why women flocked around him, yet if even only half the stories were true, flock they did. One husband, who'd been told by his wife that she had committed adultery with Calvin, had drunkenly suggested he was a hypnotist. Meegan didn't believe in hypnotism in this context, but he did believe in the power of a reputation. People tended to find what they expected to. And it was a fact that women were fatally attracted by a certain kind of infamous reputation. Because they were so certain they could resist the attraction, they had to put themselves at risk to prove their own strength? Or was it to discover and accept their own weaknesses?

The atmosphere of the island didn't help. Although it seemed impossible to pin the cause down exactly, there was something about Mallorca which bred a moral breakdown. The sun, the distance from England, the kind of isolation from harsh reality which was also experienced on a ship at sea? Or was it, more prosaically, merely the fact that the foreigners who came to live on the island were, by the very fact that they had left their homelands, footloose? Whatever the reason, proportionately more marriage beds were dishonoured on the island than anywhere in the British Isles, even in Oxshott or Sevenoaks. Had Helen spat on their marriage bed? … If only he hadn't such an active imagination, the ability to 'live' a dreamed-up situation so intently that when it was over he was as emotionally exhausted as if it had actually taken place ... If only Helen hadn't been quite so proudly independent that she bitterly resented being questioned about what she did, or if she had been ready to lie convincingly about what she had done ...

His father had often quoted the infuriating saying, 'If ifs and ands were pots and pans, there'd be no work for tinkers' hands.' His father had enthusiastically encouraged his taking up writing as a career. But then his father had been a low grade employee in an insurance office and he had visualized a writer's life as containing all the excitement he had missed ...

A car came along the spur road and he got up and walked across the patio and the baked earth to the end corner of the house. A Citroën Dyane, a battered and rusty wreck of a car, squeaked to a stop underneath the pine. Brenda Calvin opened the passenger door, which swung all the way back to clang against the bodywork, and climbed out. 'Hullo, Jim, love,' she shouted. 'We had to come up this way and I was so thirsty I said to Steve, let's take a drink off you.'

Adamson stepped out on to the drive. 'Hi, Jim! How's the world? Books doing well?'

'Graham Greene's still selling.' Meegan didn't dislike Adamson, yet neither did he really like him.

'I loved his one about the Mafia,' said Brenda.

'A book by Graham Greene?'

'It was a wonderful film. I mean the first one they made. I've seen it twice and each time felt so sad for the don.'

'Who,' said Adamson with exasperation, 'was talking about Mario Puzo?'

'I was, silly. If he wrote it. Why don't you ever listen to what I say?'

Meegan smiled. Brenda amused him — perhaps because he didn't live with her. 'Let's go and get those drinks. The sun's just about hitting the yardarm.'

'You and your stupid yardarm!' Brenda came up and kissed him loudly on both cheeks. 'You're a real square, Jim, and not at all like a proper writer. You ought to be living in a garret, eating dry crusts of bread, and singing about your tiny hand being frozen.'

'That would be a bloody silly thing to sing when the temperature's kicking a hundred,' said Adamson.

'Take no notice of Steve, Jim, he's in a terrible mood. It's all because I won't go and shriek at John for my money. But I just can't do that sort of thing.'

Adamson looked even more sullenly annoyed.

She linked her arm with Meegan's. 'Hurry up, love. If I don't pour something wet and cold down my throat in the next thirty seconds, I'm going to curl up and die. I read that one can die from dehydration.'

'You've a bit of leeway.'

She pressed her body against his. 'Now then, no nasty remarks about my size. I want you to know I weighed myself in the chemist's and their scales are dead accurate and stripped I've lost a whole kilo in the past fortnight. It's because I never have a last drink now: only the one before the last.'

'You stripped in the chemist's?'

'For God's sake, give your imagination a rest, you dirty old man. D'you think I'm going to show my treasures to that lecherous man behind the counter?'

Meegan, her arm still round his, began to walk round the house to the patio. 'Then how d'you know what you weighed stripped?'

'You really are being very trying today. I weighed myself, then took off something for my clothes.'

'How much?'

As they crossed the patio, she said: 'I'll have a long gin and tonic, sweetie, with all the ice you can cram into the glass.' She released his arm and sat down in a deck-chair. 'My God, it's so hot I'm sweating buckets. Rush that drink up.'

'You can have it as soon as you tell me how much weight you took off for your clothes.'

'You really are a swine and I can't think why I like you.' Her tone became defiant. 'Six kilos and it probably ought to be seven.'

Meegan laughed.

'You don't know what I was wearing.'

'From the look of you, it's always precious little.'

'I've always said you had X-ray eyes. Makes a girl embarrassed.' No one had ever looked less embarrassed.

Meegan turned and spoke to Adamson, who had sat down. 'What's yours, Steve?'

'I could murder a brandy and soda.'

Meegan left the patio and went into the sitting-room and across to the wooden chest in which they kept their bottles. He poured out three drinks, added ice, put some olives on a plate, and carried the tray outside.

'Where's Helen?' asked Brenda, as he handed her the gin and tonic.

'She went out in the car earlier on.'

'Then it was her we saw going up the Laraix valley. I said it was, but Steve argued blind it wasn't. He's been arguing about everything since he got up this morning. Even tried to tell me that Bangkok is the capital of Thailand.'

'It is.'

'No, it isn't. It's the capital of Siam. I learned that at school.'

'It's the same country.'

'For God's sake! … Why can't they make up their minds where they live?'

Meegan handed Adamson the brandy and soda.

'I waved like crazy at Helen, but she didn't answer. I wonder why not? We'd been up to see Violet and Harry. Did you know she's thinking of returning to England to live?'

'Violet? She can't be: the taxes would kill her.'

'Stephanie. She says she can't take the mañanas any longer and wants to live in a country where at least some of the things get done properly. I just don't understand her fuss. I think it's the way nothing happens when it should, or does when it shouldn't, that absolutely makes this place. I mean, if you must have things done exactly on time, become an engine driver. Like Perce.'

'Perce Goldstein isn't an engine driver and never has been,' snapped Adamson.

'Who said anything that daft? You're going to have to stop drinking if you get that confused. I was talking about a Perce I used to know — George Hamish.'

'Oh, my God!' muttered Adamson.

Meegan sat down. Had Brenda realized that her husband lived along the Laraix road and that it was unlikely Helen could have been going to see anyone else along there?

*

Breeden, in the Seat 600 he'd hired at the airport twelve days before, looked briefly out of the side window. He saw a drystone wall and beyond that a field under intense cultivation with crops of peppers, aubergines, beans, lettuces, artichokes, tomatoes, and trefoil, being grown under the shade of algarroba, orange, and almond trees. There was an air of unwholesome excess about the land, he thought. How much nicer his garden in England was with its neatly mown lawn, its round rose-beds, and the crazy-paving path which he had laid that spring. He hoped his sister, who had lived with him since she had been widowed, had remembered to use the long-lasting weedkiller — at the right strength — on the path, if necessary. And was she watering the roses if the ground was too dry?

He saw the dirt track off to the left, by the twisted fig tree, and he slowed down and turned into it. The Seat bounced up and down on the rough surface. In England, he thought, with conscious superiority, one did not have to suffer pot-holed dirt tracks to visit a house. This island was, as he had known it would be, archaic.

He came to an old man who was laboriously cutting long grass on the wide verge with an equally old sickle and who spat into the dust when the car was abreast of him. Breeden knew a moment of sharp irritation, judging the gesture to have been a personal demonstration of hatred towards the foreigner — completely forgetting that it was unlikely the old man could have seen him clearly enough to have identified him as one.

Ca'n Adeane had its nameboard on a wooden pole in the right-hand grass verge. There was an elaborate wrought-iron gate, set in a sandstone wall, and he had to get out and open this: in the heat, in the suit he was wearing, every movement brought out fresh sweat. He felt damp and stickily dirty. Without consciously formulating that fact, he decided he'd make Calvin jump through the hoop.

A track, which ran along the north side of the rectangular field, led up to the house. This was old, with metre-thick walls of honey-grey stone, variegated brown-tiled roof, green wooden shutters, and a patio over which, spread out across a wire framework supported by stone pillars, was a massive vine from which hung dozens of bunches of well formed grapes. Nothing like a Kent or Sussex yeoman's cottage.

As he stopped in the turning circle at the end of the track, a man stepped out of the front door on to the patio and, coming to a halt under the shade of the vine, studied Breeden.

Breeden, briefcase in his hand, walked over. 'Mr Calvin?'

'That's right.' Calvin shook hands with a firm grip. He was the same size as Breeden, but there was in all his movements a suggestion of hard physical condition. He was dressed as casually as Breeden was dressed formally, yet there could be no doubt who wore the better quality clothes: his open-neck shirt and green slacks had the unmistakable style of expensive tailoring and material. His face was squarish, a little uneven in features, with eyes wide apart, a nose which was patrician in form, and a mouth which was notable for very full lips. When he smiled, the lines about the corners of his mouth gathered together into an expression of mocking good humour suggesting he was a man who never quite accepted anything at face value, but was always ready for a delayed banana-skin. He had a casually self-confident manner, of the kind that forced respect from porters and headwaiters. 'And you will be Mr Breeden, from the Bank of England, hot on the scent of corruption?'

'How did you know who I was?'

'My dear fellow, since you landed on the island the sole topic of conversation at drinks has been the trail of havoc you've left behind you. You've even gained the ultimate expression of an Englishman's respect, a nick-name. The Fifth Horseman.'

'The Fifth Horseman?' queried Breeden, knowing he was being slow, yet forced against his will to ask.

'Riding stirrup to stirrup with war, famine, plague, and death.'

Breeden was used to being received with dislike, even fear, but not mockery. He felt uneasy, as if he had lost his bearings, and because of this he showed an unusual degree of open hostility. 'Mr Calvin, I want to speak to you.'

'The circumstances being what they are, I rather imagined that. Come on in and have a drink and throw off some of those clothes you're wearing or you'll pass out.'

'I'm quite all right, thank you,' he answered stiffly.

'Suit yourself, as the polar bear said to the Mexican Hairless … Excuse my going first and mind your head on the lintels: this country wasn't made for six-footers.'

The interior of the house disturbed Breeden. It was all too much … too decadent came to mind when he saw a blown-up Beardsley print. They went through the hall and under a low archway into the high-roofed sitting-room and it seemed to him that everywhere there were Persian carpets, tapestries, paintings, prints, pieces of beautifully inlaid furniture, porcelain figurines, icons, gold and silver snuffboxes, velvet chairs, startlingly coloured cushions … He sat down in an armchair, pressed his knees firmly together, and rested his briefcase on them.

'What is it to be?' asked Calvin, who remained standing. 'A liqueur since we're not long since lunch, or a brandy or gin since we're not far short of drinking time?'

'Nothing for me, thank you. I seldom drink.'

'Very wise. But that surely makes for a constricted life on an island where the only other forms of popular entertainment are sun, sea and sex?'

To his chagrin, Breeden felt himself blushing slightly, as if he were a callow youth.

Calvin crossed the room, walking round the tiger skin — the head snarled with great malevolence — and went to a beautifully made cocktail cabinet with intricately designed brass hinges and locking plate. He poured himself out a generous brandy, closed the cabinet door, and returned to the centre of the room where he sat on a tapestry-covered low chair. He raised the glass with his left hand. 'Here's mud in your eyes. And lots of it when you're really hot on the trail.'

Breeden coughed. 'Mr Calvin ... '

'John. No one uses surnames out here.'

'I prefer to use surnames, thank you.'

'No fraternization with the enemy?'

'Mr Calvin, I have been sent to Mallorca by the Bank of England to investigate certain matters which are concerned with illegal transfer of capital out of Britain by British subjects. Under the Exchange Act of nineteen ... '

'Don't you think it's far too hot for all that?'

'I wish to make certain facts perfectly clear. Under the act of nineteen forty-seven ... '

'If you insist on running through the law, let's paraphrase and save time. Anyone under sixty-five may not take more than five thousand out without paying the dollar premium until four years after he's emigrated. If he does and Big Brother catches him, he can be fined up to three times the premium he's evaded. To pay the fine, all existing assets in the UK can be forcibly encashed. How's that for an amateur assessment?'

'Within limits, Mr Calvin, what you say is sufficiently accurate ... '

'Only qualified approval? What is it? Don't you like amateurs horning in?'

'Do you understand the full meaning of the relevant sections of the act?'

'I'll confess to having been so intrigued by them as to wonder what sort of twisted mind could conceive them. The righteousness of the genuine bureaucrat has always frightened me: any man who can believe that what he's doing is utterly right is a terrifying phenomenon.'

'There have to be laws,' said Breeden defensively.

'But by what alchemy of logic does a righteous man help to impose oppressive laws and yet not see himself as an oppressor?'

'What's wrong with saying a person musn't take out more than five thousand pounds from the UK without paying a premium? The country can't be drained of capital.'

'It's the mentality that's so wrong. It's not other people's money the emigrant wants to take out of the country, it's his own. Deny him that right and you're dictating how he can enjoy his own possessions. That makes you a dictator. And dictators haven't ever etched their names in history as bywords for liberality and geniality.'

'Mr Calvin, I know what the law is — I might point out that I am in no way responsible for its form — and when it is broken ... '

'You come hot under the collar to see me. Why? Have I broken the law? And if I have, can any practical steps be taken to bring home to me the enormity of my behaviour?' Calvin drank some brandy. 'Being an essentially practical sort of a bloke, I'd say it would pay you to examine the second question first. After all, what's the good of calling a man a bastard if you can't produce his shortened birth certificate to prove it? ... Now I am without any assets in the UK. Lamentable from your point of view, but very forward thinking from mine. Without assets to impound, what can you do? The offences under your beloved act are non-extraditable.'

'Offences are, under sub-section one, non-extraditable as you say.'

'Disappointed?'

'I do my work without allowing personal emotions to intrude.'

'Highly commendable.'

'Mr Calvin, during the course of my investigations, I have discovered that several people on this island have exported money illegally from the United Kingdom — by which I mean ... '

'I know what you mean.'

'Very well. Perhaps you also realize that some of these people still have assets in the UK?'

'You'll have to put that down to the incorrigible British vice of amateurism.'

Breeden tried to regain his normal sense of pleasurable superiority. He looked slowly round the room. 'This house and its contents must represent a very great deal of money, yet your records show that officially you have not exported a single pound. Would you care to say how you've acquired this house?'

'I bought it.'

'Do you understand that the Bank of England is empowered to investigate … '

'Anything that takes its fancy in the United Kingdom, but nothing outside it, to the mortification of all internationally-minded bureaucrats. And out here the Spanish banks have a wonderful sense of bank secrecy. Ask them about my accounts and they'll smile and shrug their shoulders.'

Breeden could not conceal his sense of triumph. 'Maybe. But banks do not happen to be the sole source of information. I've been talking to English people who've been very forthcoming.'

Calvin raised his eyebrows. 'What's happened to the tradition of the silent upper lip?'

'Some of those who have broken the law have assets still in the UK and they're very frightened at the prospect of losing such assets. They've been quite ready to tell me how their money has been illegally shifted out here.'

'Have you really been exercising a little blackmail? Has the Old Lady of Threadneedle Street taken to harlotry?'

'My job,' said Breeden very stiffly, 'is to discover who has been breaking the law. Mr Calvin, you have illegally transferred, to my knowledge, a considerable sum of money from the United Kingdom to here for three different people.'

'I want to make one thing quite clear. I've always done it for a clear ten per cent. I am not a charitable organization.' 'The act of smuggling out money for others, Mr Calvin — Perhaps you never got so far in your reading of the Act? — under section sixty-three, sub-section one, is an arrestable offence, punishable by up to ten years' imprisonment and a heavy fine. Further, it is an extraditable offence.'

Calvin yawned.

'You arranged with an import/export firm in England that they would be paid large sums of money. They invoiced for the export of machinery although, of course, no machinery was ever exported to Spain. The firm kept the money and used it in the normal course of business in the UK while authorizing their Spanish branch to pay out in Spain, in pesetas, ninety per cent of the amount it had received. You collected the pesetas and paid them to the person concerned, less your ten per cent.'

'Quite right. It's all quite simple, really, once the paperwork's been sorted out. I didn't invent the system, of course, but I am quite proud of the way I refined its method of execution.'

'The Bank of England will instruct the Director of Public Prosecutions to take proceedings against you.'

'And the DPP will discover from the police that nobody but myself knows the name of the export/import firm since I always paid the money in at one end and always received it at the other. It's quite impossible exhaustively to investigate every firm which might be guilty and in any case I pride myself on the effectiveness of the paperwork involved. In the end the DPP, who surely has to be a practical man by nature, will undoubtedly declare a … Is it a *nolle prosequi*?'

'I do not know. But, Mr Calvin, you have overlooked the obvious fact that there will be movements of money through your accounts corresponding to the dates I've been given … '

'In England, I naturally dealt in cash. Out here, accounts are secret to an investigating Englishman.'

'The Spanish authorities will co-operate in a criminal matter.'

'But first you have to furnish them with the proof that I am a criminal. And how can you do that without access to the accounts?'

Breeden began to tap with his fingers on the briefcase.

'Give up,' said Calvin cheerfully, 'and concentrate for the rest of your stay on having a real holiday … How much longer are you here?'

'I am leaving for Nice next week,' said Breeden very stiffly.

'More unfortunate clients, unknowingly awaiting the pleasure of meeting you?'

'I have certain persons both here and there whom I shall be interviewing.'

'And you hope to learn something that will nail me down, once and for all? Forget it. I've always looked after my own skin with the care of a dedicated hypochondriac. Relax, now, and have a drink and to hell with duty.'

Breeden stood up. 'I think I'd better leave.'

'Really? Just before you go, then, how d'you like the sound of five thousand pounds, paid into a Swiss account in your name and number?'

Breeden's thin-lipped mouth tightened.

'Incorruptible? Your sentiments do you tremendous credit, but on this island they're likely to make you feel rather lonely: corruption is the only common bond between many of us. Never mind. I'll try not to think too harshly of you — a man can't easily learn to be weaker than his upbringing and environment have made him.'

Breeden hurried out of the room and the house of corruption and decadence.

CHAPTER VI

Meegan was listening to Strauss's *Don Juan* when Helen entered the house and came past the kitchen door to the sitting-room. He stared at her, but said nothing, and after one brief, troubled look at him she went back to the passage which led off to the bedrooms and bathrooms. She returned and sat down as the music came to an end. He stood up and crossed to the playing unit.

'When I listen to any of his music I always feel as if my emotions were being stretched to their limits,' she said.

He turned the record over. 'What was it like?'

'Like any other cocktail party out here, except that the Blagdons know fewer interesting people and one daren't drink their gin because they buy the cheapest firewater and fill their Gordon's bottles with it … I wish you'd come.'

'I told you, I wasn't in the mood.'

'But you ought to get out and about much more … '

'You don't think one wanderer in the family is enough?'

'Jim,' she said quietly, but firmly, 'we've got to talk.'

He started *Till Eulenspiegel* playing, then sat down. 'All right, let's talk. Was John there?'

'Of course. You know he's friendly with Martha and George.'

'And that's why you insisted on going, even though you always describe Martha as the bitch goddess?'

'I needed to get right away from the supercharged atmosphere of this house.'

'Then you didn't want me to go with you, did you?'

'For Heaven's sake! Not even you could keep it up at a cocktail party — not after the fourth drink.' Her gaze softened and her tone warmed. 'Jim, stop being such a fool and take time off to remember I love you.'

He stared at her, his face working. 'Do you? Didn't you go to his house yesterday?'

'Yes.'

'Why?'

47

'He invited me. And you'd … you'd been so bitter towards me, I went as a kind of stupid retaliation, I suppose.'

'He oozed charm?' His voice was now harsh.

'Oozed is a very fair description.'

'And you fell for it and … and … ' He stopped, unable to ask the final question.

'No, I didn't go to bed with him. Don't you know me better than that? If I had betrayed you, I'd have come back and told you yesterday, face to face.'

He longed to believe her, yet knew too much doubt to do so. The mocking theme of the music seemed to underline his doubt.

*

In the early hours of Tuesday, there was a violent storm. The thunder, which had been growling somewhere back in the mountains, grew violently louder as lightning speared the sky: one bolt struck the lightning conductor on the hermitage perched high up on its conical hill. Rain fell with torrential force, drumming on roofs so loudly that to those in the houses it sounded as if Olympian oceans of water were being emptied over them: three minutes after the storm first hit Llueso, the lights went out as the electricity failed.

The torrente which bordered the eastern side of Llueso, a boulder-strewn dry gulch the previous day, began to run, soon with a savage force as the earth-stained water lashed its way down to the sea.

*

Alvarez drove out of Llueso at half past eight, crossing over the still running torrente — the level was now right down — and turned left on to the Laraix road. He passed two large houses, owned by foreigners, and the garden centre, whose trade was almost exclusively with foreigners, and then stopped opposite a field in which a couple of dozen hobbled sheep and three hobbled goats were feeding. He lit a cigarette. All the foreigners in the world couldn't prevent the miracle of rain, he thought with quiet satisfaction. The land was baked dry, the grass seemingly dead, leaves of the orange trees curled, plants drooped despite intensive irrigation … Came the rain and the land swelled, the grass grew green, the orange tree leaves straightened, plants grew tall and proud, and the air was filled with the heady scent of rebirth. He looked up at the mountains, not yet dried out so that they appeared dark and ominous, and saw three vultures soaring in the thermals. He smiled with simple pleasure.

He returned to his car and drove on, to reach the dirt track off to the left, down which he went with complete indifference to the tortured squeals of the sorely tried suspension. When he reached Ca'n Adeane, he parked immediately in front of the ornate gate.

He walked down the drive. There were vines trained along the sandstone wall and the bunches were heavy although not quite ripe: someone knew how to prune and tend vines. In the first half of the field were tomatoes, peppers, climbing beans, and lettuces: someone knew how to cultivate the land. Not the Englishman, that was for sure. The second half of the field was stubble and from the bareness of the earth about the stalks it was clear it had been closely gleaned after the corn had been cut — more proof that the place was not farmed by the Englishman: foreigners were indifferent to waste. He reached the house and because it was not owned by an islander he did not step inside before calling out, but knocked on the opened door.

Calvin came through the fly screen. Alvarez introduced himself. Calvin, showing neither astonishment nor the slightest apprehension, shook hands and said: 'Come in and have some coffee. I was just making some for myself.'

Alvarez went in and through to the sitting-room, intrigued by the bizarre furnishings, yet seeing in them only a desire to be different, not the strong smell of decadence which Breeden had found.

'Can I offer you anything to eat?' asked Calvin.

'Thank you, señor, but a coffee would be quite enough.'

'You'll take it with a cognac, though?'

'That would be very pleasant.'

Calvin was gone from the room for some ten minutes. When he returned he carried a tray on which were two cups of coffee, sugar, milk, and two glasses of brandy. 'The Mallorquin breakfast is one of the local habits I immediately turned to with tremendous enthusiasm: especially after a heavy night.' He held the tray for Alvarez to help himself.

Alvarez took sugar but not milk. 'We have a saying, señor: "Start the day on a cognac and the sun will shine before eleven."' He drank some coffee, then tipped the brandy into the cup and stirred with a spoon.

Calvin sat down. 'So what brings you all the way out here at breakfast-time? Something very pressing?'

'It is a matter which has to be dealt with, although I, señor, would perhaps not describe it as pressing. My enquiries have to do with the smuggling of American cigarettes and watches into this island in large quantities.'

'Really? You surprise me. I didn't think that went on these days.'

'There's always been a little.' Alvarez shrugged his thickset shoulders. 'Our fishermen welcome both the profit and the excitement. But unfortunately it seems that the quantity of smuggling has now become very large: so large that much of what comes in is being sent on to the Peninsula, which is easy, of course, as there are no customs.'

'You know, now I think about it, I suppose I have been offered more American cigarettes than usual in the past few months. I'm a great fan of Chesterfields and a lot of people know that ... I wonder if the ones I've been buying have been smuggled? I'll show you a pack and maybe you can tell me.' He stood up and crossed to the walnut roll-top desk, opened a drawer, and brought out a pack of cigarettes.

Alvarez looked very briefly at the top of the pack. 'Yes, señor, that has been smuggled. It bears no government seal.'

'Well, I'll be damned! I was going to offer you one — does it mean that now you mustn't accept?'

'From a practical point of view, since the smuggling has taken place I can't see that if I smoke one of the cigarettes I will be affecting anything.'

Calvin smiled as he opened one end of the top and tapped out a couple of cigarettes, before offering the pack. 'I wish all authority adopted so sensible an attitude.' He flicked open a lighter and lit the detective's cigarette, returned to his seat.

Alvarez finished his coffee. 'Señor, permit me to explain simply why I am here now. As I told you, much smuggling is going on and that means the smugglers on the island have had to find much money because the trade does not work on credit. The fishermen who usually smuggle do not have big money — if they did, they would not be fishermen. So someone has provided the big money and I think that person is a foreigner.'

'Why should you think that?'

'We are a small island with people who have always been honest until the foreigners came. Even now, the dishonest islanders are only the ones who have to deal with foreigners and they are only a little dishonest. Except where a man loses his temper, there is nothing. A little smuggling is nothing. But a lot of smuggling is something.'

'You obviously don't like foreigners?'

'In my job, señor, I neither specially like nor dislike them.'

'But you're not reluctant to heap the responsibility for trouble on their shoulders?'

'I can only speak from my very limited experience and that tells me who does the stealing and who brings in drugs.'

'No doubt it all depends on one's point of view. Anyway, let's move from the general to the specific. You reckon there's a lot of smuggling going on and it's being financed by a wealthy foreigner. Believing that, why come here to talk to me about it? Surely you don't imagine I can help?'

'Señor, as a detective I have to study every possibility that is suggested to me, no matter how impossible I, personally, may think it.'

'And I come within the category of a possibility?'

'Your name has been given to me as that of the man who has supplied the money for the big smuggling.'

'You've got to be joking!'

'Señor, I try never to joke when I am working because other people do not always understand my sense of humour.'

'Well, I wish the rumour were true. Then, by definition, I'd be a rich man. Instead of someone who has a hell of a job coping with inflation, a dropping pound, and an extravagant wife whose friends all have very expensive tastes.'

Alvarez looked briefly round the room. 'But you are not poor, señor?'

'Churchill defined poverty as the moment at which you could no longer afford a bottle of champagne every morning at eleven … You're trying to judge by the contents of this house? Merely a reminder of life when inflation was German history, the pound stood proud, and my wife and I still struggled to find sufficient in common to continue living together.'

'Then you can assure me you have provided no money for the smuggling?'

'My only contribution has been the unwitting purchase of smuggled cigarettes, such as the pack I've just offered you.'

'And if that were a crime, señor, half the population would have to be arrested.'

'Exactly. Now how about another coffee and cognac before you go?'

'Thank you, no. We have another saying: "Start the day on two cognacs and by twelve the sun will be too hot."'

Calvin laughed. 'And there's more truth than usual in that one … Well, I hope you manage to find out who's been doing all the smuggling, but I'll be sorry if all the American cigarettes go off the market. I'm afraid the one local product I've never come to terms with is the black tobacco.' When he saw Alvarez was not moving, he stood up, slightly irritated that the detective didn't have the nous to know when to go. 'I'm very sorry, but I'm really rather busy this morning and I have a friend coming here later on to discuss a spot of bother he's in.'

Alvarez studied his own shoes, which were heavy and clumsy-looking. 'Señor, the banker — that is what I shall call him — must have been handling large sums of money.'

'I suppose so. But … '

'He would need very large sums to pay out to the people who deliver the cigarettes and watches, he would receive even larger sums when they are sold to the next people in the line. So it should be easy to know who could be the banker by seeing what large money he has been handling.'

'And how would you go about that?'

'In the usual way. I would study the person's style of living and his bank accounts.'

Calvin sat down again. His voice became edged with sarcasm. 'You don't think that a foreigner who went into the smuggling racket would deal in cash and his profits would be moved smartly out of the country so that if suspicion ever did fall on him there wouldn't be any record of the money movements to trap him?'

'It is forbidden to take large sums of money out of Spain, señor.'

'Forbidden by law, but aren't we talking about a man who's laughing at the law? All he'll do is book to fly out of Spain, load his suitcase with peseta notes, and check in at the airport. The luggage is never searched. He arrives at the other end, collects his suitcase and the fortune, and walks away.'

'And then?'

'He banks it. You must know about Swiss numbered accounts which were tailored for this sort of operation?'

'I have heard about them, señor,' said Alvarez vaguely. 'But is it really quite so simple? When a man has a lot of cash, he sometimes spends a little of it right away, in a kind of celebration, and then perhaps he doesn't need to draw his usual money from the bank. Do you see what I am thinking?'

'No, I don't.'

'I am thinking, señor, that if you will tell me where your bank account is, I will investigate it. Then, when I see there are no large sums of money and no times when no money is drawn, I can tell my superior that Señor Calvin has nothing to do with smuggling.'

When Calvin next spoke, his voice had lost its note of amused condescension. 'I've told you I've nothing to do with smuggling and that ought to be enough. And bank accounts in this country are secret.'

'The police always have the right of investigation. Surely it is the same in England?'

'Only when a court has authorized it.'

'We also have certain formalities. Naturally, I would observe them.'

'You want to call me a liar?'

'Señor! Of course I have no such wish. You have given me your word and that is quite sufficient for me. The word of an Englishman! My parents taught me what that means. But my superior comes from Madrid and is not really a gentleman in such matters. And he must be convinced. Surely you would wish me to convince him?'

Calvin lit a cigarette. There was now a hard, wary look on his face and his voice was crisp. He inhaled, blew out the smoke in four perfect smoke rings, then said: 'Obviously, I'd better explain something.'

'I am hoping we will have no misunderstandings.'

'The fact is, there have been fairly large amounts passing through my account, but these have absolutely nothing to do with smuggling. They are solely concerned with financial arrangements I make for certain English people.'

'Would you be kind enough to explain them, rather simply so that I can understand?'

'You must have heard that an Englishman can't ship out of England as much money as he wants without paying a very high premium? I move it out here for a much lesser premium. As far as Spanish law is concerned, I'm doing nothing wrong.'

'And by English law?'

'Since England has little use for democracy these days, it's illegal. So perhaps now you can understand the situation? Money has been paid into and out of my account, but these sums aren't in any way tied up with smuggling.'

'Then once you have proved where the money came from, señor, it can be forgotten.'

'Proved?'

'You will naturally wish to prove the truth of what you say.'

'How am I supposed to do that, for Pete's sake?'

'Most easily, by identifying where the money in your account came from, who paid it to you, and who you paid it to.'

'Look, you haven't really understood my position. I can't start proving I did bring the money out from the UK, or the authorities at home will begin to learn what I've been up to.'

'But you are in Spain.'

'For me, it's an extraditable offence.'

Alvarez rubbed his heavy chin. 'I can see your problem now, señor, but most unfortunately I shall need absolute proof that the money came from England — and by what means. Perhaps I can proceed on my own and let you be silent? We have very friendly relations with the British police and I am sure they will co-operate.'

'For God's sake ... Calvin struggled to keep his temper in check. 'I've told you, the moment the English police learn what's on, they'll grab me.'

'But if that is the case, how are we ever to prove the facts?'

'Surely common sense will tell you that no one in his right senses would put money made from smuggling through his bank account ... ?'

Alvarez spoke so blandly that it was impossible to judge whether he realized the full import of his words. 'Señor, some criminals become so clever that sometimes they overlook the obvious.' He stood up. 'Perhaps you will consider the matter and then telephone me at the post in Llueso. I shall need the name of your bank — all your banks: and please don't become distressed when I tell you that I shall have to speak to every bank on the island to make certain you have not forgotten some small, insignificant account.' He held out his hand. 'Goodbye, señor, and thank you very much for the coffee and cognac. I hope that between us we find a solution for your problems.'

He left. Life, he thought, occasionally had its compensations.

CHAPTER VII

Alvarez's bedroom faced south. After he'd woken up in the morning he liked to open the shutters and then return to bed and stare out through the window, across the roofs of other houses, at Puig Llueso on the crown of which stood the several buildings which had once been a hermitage but which were now looked after by nuns. The bones of Santa Antonia were housed in a small casket in the chapel and when his cousin's son had been so terribly ill and the doctor had been able to do nothing for the terrified boy, he had walked up the track to the chapel and had prayed to Santa Antonia. Within twenty-four hours, the boy had begun to mend. The doctor, of course, had claimed that the antibiotics had worked the cure: doctors were greedy in all things. It had been a miracle. And because it had been a miracle, he had returned to the shrine, completing the last three hundred metres on his knees, and he had knelt again before Santa Antonia's bones and he had thanked her, with tears brimming down his cheeks.

He lay in his bed and stared at Puig Llueso, but his thoughts were elsewhere. Today was Thursday, and so there were only three more full working days until Sunday. Often on Sundays he went off into the country in his car and had a solitary picnic, usually in a field. This habit tended to upset his cousin, who believed in the traditional family Sunday meal, but the solitary picnics in the countryside offered him a spiritual rejuvenation. He came from the soil and longed to return to the soil. He knew exactly the kind of house he was going to retire to. It wouldn't be modernized and it wouldn't have electricity or running water — far too expensive — but it would be old and built of rock, its tiles would be weathered and held down by stones, it would have a donkey well which he would restore, and it would have land right round it. Rich, friable, red-brown loam which gave a man's hands more pleasure than a woman's naked flank.

The telephone rang.

He swore, then looked at his watch. Only eight o'clock, yet someone was demanding to pour out a load of troubles and then to leave him with the job of clearing them up. God had erred when he had created the human race with sufficient imagination to invent the telephone. He reached across to the receiver and lifted it. 'Yes?'

'It's the post here, Enrique. We've just had an Englishwoman in and she was damn near hysterical.'

'Why bother me? Call a doctor.'

'Come off it, you lazy bastard … Her Spanish was grim, but if we understood it anything like right, she says that an Englishman, by the name of Calvin, has committed suicide.'

'D'you say Calvin?'

'That's right.'

'I'll get right over. Hold her until I arrive.'

'Hold her yourself. She's already gone, faster'n a bat out of hell. Said she had to get back to her own house before her husband returned.'

'She's been busy, then?'

'She's English, so what d'you expect?'

'I don't know that I expect anything. What's her name?'

'Ormond. O-R-M-O-N-D.'

'Where's she live?'

'On the Llueso/Playa Nueva road at Ca'n Ormond. But she said no one's to go if her husband's there.'

'How are we supposed to know if he is, or isn't?'

'That's your worry, mate, not mine.'

Once the call was over, Alvarez climbed out of bed and walked along the passage to the bathroom, where he had a quick shower. Then he dressed and went downstairs. His cousin was in the kitchen and she poured him out a bowlful of soup, still hot from having been warmed up for her husband who had just gone out to work, and cut him a thick slice of bread. She was obviously curious about the cause of his hurry, but when he said nothing she left to start cleaning the sitting-room, by now well used to his silent, secretive manner.

His car was parked immediately outside the front door. He drove to the end of the road, turned right and later right again and this brought him to the bridge over the torrente — now dry, with the stones on the bed bleached white so that there might not have been any rain in months. Beyond the bridge was the Laraix road.

In the sunshine, still with a quality of softness in it because the heat was not yet intense, Ca'n Adeane looked beautiful, a natural part of the land. He opened the ornate gate and drove down the track, past the vines, parking in the circular turning point. Any man who owned this place and committed suicide was a fool, no matter what the pressures.

The wooden front door, with its cat hole, was open, moving almost imperceptibly to the very slight breeze. He parted the fly curtain and tried the handle of the glass-fronted door. It turned and he pushed the door open, stepped into the hall. He called out. There was no response and he went into the sitting-room, through to the dining-room, back into the hall and from there into the kitchen. There was no sign of Calvin, drunk or sober, dead or alive. There was one further room to the side of the kitchen and this was clearly used as a study: there were bookshelves half filled with books, odd cases which looked as if no other home could be found for them, a long table on which was a typewriter and a litter of books and papers, and against the far wall a glass-fronted gun cupboard. This was empty of guns.

Upstairs, there were three bedrooms and one bathroom. One of the bedrooms was large, with a double bed, and it was furnished as exotically as the sitting-room downstairs with, amongst other things, two paintings of nudes which made Alvarez purse his lips because he was a great believer in discretion. The other two bedrooms were much smaller, each containing only a single bed, and they had the air of rooms very seldom used. There was no body in any of them nor, looking through the windows, could he see a body lying on the ground outside. Why had Señora Ormond been hysterically convinced that Calvin had committed suicide?

He returned downstairs and went out and round to the back of the house. For twenty metres there was rough grass, then there were trees, part of a belt which ran parallel with the road. He crossed the grass and went in amongst the trees, a typical mixture of pine, evergreen oak, and a thick shrub layer of maquis. Five metres on was the torrente which ran past Llueso and he checked that Calvin was not lying on its bed. Would the señora have climbed down into the torrente, with its somewhat precipitous side and boulder-strewn bottom, and then climbed up the equally precipitous far side to search for the missing man? He doubted it. Nor did he think she would have gone very far in either direction through the belt of trees since the undergrowth could cause quite painful scratches.

He returned to the house. Somewhere, something had alerted Señora Ormond. What? The hall and sitting-room were bare of alarms. There was nothing in the dining-room. In the study he went round the table to check the papers on the top and that was when he noticed for the first time the typewritten note which was wound into position, with the beginning of the note a few lines clear of the roller. He pulled it free and read it.

Will whoever first reads this please call the police.

I am going to commit suicide and if all goes to plan my manly beauty will be somewhat marred in the process. However, I have always understood that the police are used to gruesome sights and will therefore not be unduly disturbed by my mortal remains.

My reasons for suicide are simply explained: I feel an explanation is necessary as most people still suffer under the delusion that a person has to be at least partially insane to kill himself and I would like to be remembered — should anyone take the bother — as sane. Ulysses avoided the Sirens by deafening his crew and having himself tied to the mast, but I am less resourceful and can see no way out of the untenable position in which I suddenly find myself. (The fact that I can only save myself from one peril not at all of my making by falling into the clutches of another which is, holds an irony which at other times I should find amusing.)

I believe that under Spanish law at least part of my estate has to go to my wife and the fact that we are separated is of no consequence. In any case, under my will she is my sole beneficiary. I truly hope that on the sale of my house and its contents she will receive enough money to replace the capital I received from her at the beginning of our married life.

The English community has a habit of showing the flag — should I write shroud? — and attending the funeral of a compatriot, irrespective of the past (a chequered past on the part of the victim always seems to bring out the greatest number of mourners: perhaps because the merit of their presence is even more satisfying to themselves?). I should prefer no such hypocritical display. Those who disliked me should feel absolutely free to continue to dislike my memory: I would, being magnanimous in my final hour, offer them a measure of consolation — no man could be as successful in the pursuit of love as rumour has had me.

I have no intention of apologizing to Brenda for the past — but in proof of the fact that I have always had her welfare to heart, if not to hand, I offer her some sound advice. Invest her money where she cannot easily get at it. She is far too generous with all she possesses.

Alvarez dropped the signed paper on to the typewriter. He brought a pack of cigarettes from his pocket and lit one. He was shocked. When a man was preparing to face his Maker, he should at least show some respect for the proprieties.

*

Ca'n Ormond was an old finca which had recently been so extensively modernized and altered that now only from the north, or mountain side, was it possible to realize what the building had once been. There was a swimming pool to the south and on one side of this was a small complex with covered eating area, barbecue pit, bar, and one changing room. The garden had been laid out with far too much precision, but because of extensive watering the plants had grown with such lush vigour that they sprawled out of their beds to mask boundaries and in doing so had brought life to the scene.

Alvarez crossed to what appeared to be the front door — from the car there had been a choice of three — and he rang the bell. A maid, in neat white and blue checked apron, opened the door. 'Is the señora in?'

The maid, middle-aged, with a face that looked scarred but wasn't, said: 'She isn't feeling very well, so you can't ... '

'Cuerpo de Policia. It's an important matter.'

'Oh!' She looked at him with uneasy surprise. 'You'd better come in, then. I'll tell her you're here.'

He was shown into a sitting/dining-room, L-shaped with the dining-room in the short arm of the L and separated by two elegantly curved arches. He knew little about furniture, yet was certain that the various inlaid pieces, with the patina of age and care, were valuable. The three paintings on the far wall each had above a strip light and the silver on the large side table in the dining-room was elegant and plentiful. The Persian carpets were very lustrous. No need to wonder if they were rich.

The maid came down the stairs to say that Señora Ormond would be with him as soon as possible. He sat down in a tapestry-covered chair and waited. If he were rich, he wouldn't live in a house like this, even though he could appreciate its elegance — he'd live in a plain house and use his money to buy land and more land, so that he could tramp it each day and revel in its possession, as a miser counted and recounted his gold.

Mrs Ormond entered the room some fifteen minutes later. He guessed her age at the middle thirties. She was dressed with great care and chic and her hair was piled up in bouffant style. Her face was round and regular and beautiful in a childish sense, unmarked by any sharp lines of character: right then, she was clearly frightened. She spoke with a rush of words, interrupting him as he began to introduce himself. 'I said you must ring up to see if my husband were back.' She looked fearfully at the drive, visible through the large picture windows.

'I'm sorry, señora, but the matter is too urgent.'

'But he said he'd be back by eleven.' She looked at her diamond-studded watch. 'If they get back early ...'

'Early from where, señora?'

'Mike sailed with Bill to Menorca. He said they'd be back in the Port by eleven because Bill's flying home this afternoon. If Bill sailed in early ... '

'Señora, let me ask you the few questions I must, as quickly as possible. Then I will leave.'

She looked at him, her face working. 'Did you ... Is it true?'

'I have searched the house and the land, but I have found nothing. Can you tell me ... '

She interrupted him again. 'I was worried sick and I ran into the house and called out and there wasn't a sound. I looked for him and even though it wasn't a day for the maid his bed was made up and since he could never be bothered to make it himself that meant he couldn't have slept in it. Then I found that note in the typewriter. Oh God! He can't have done it. He's got to be joking, hasn't he?' she appealed with desperation.

'Why were you originally worried about him, señora?'

'Because we'd arranged everything, but when I phoned there wasn't any answer ... '

With quiet, tactful questioning, he managed to persuade her to tell the story in some sort of chronological order. Ormond had told his wife two days before that they had been invited on a twenty-two-hour trip to Menorca and back. She, on the pretext of being so bad a sailor, had refused to go: when she'd spoken to Calvin, they'd arranged to meet whilst her husband was away. (Alvarez tried hard not to show his sharp disapproval of all her actions: although a man of considerable compassion, he would not have been sorry to see the husband drive through the gates whilst he was still there so that explanations would have been inevitable. Women's morals should be beyond suspicion.)

The moment her husband could be assumed to be safely at sea, she had telephoned Calvin's home. There had been no answer. Throughout the day she had gone on telephoning, always without success, and she'd become more and more worried that something had happened to him. By the time she'd gone to bed, she'd convinced herself he must be in trouble and during the night, when she slept very badly, trouble in her mind turned into tragedy. (Women's minds — English women's minds, that was — were not only born to deceive others, they were also born to deceive themselves: why hadn't she considered the possibility of Calvin's having found himself another and more stimulating woman for the night?)

She hadn't been able to go to Ca'n Adeane too early in the morning — her visit must seem to be above board. (English hypocrisy at its starkest.) In the house she'd found the bed made and, terrified, she'd pictured the accident up in the mountains with his car rolling over and over down the side of a precipitous slope ... She'd found the suicide note and the shock had all but killed her.

'When did you last see the señor, señora?'

'Just before Mike told me about the boat trip. I can't see him very often as Mike gets so jealous.'

But clearly not jealous enough. 'And had you heard from him since?'

'The agreement was that I'd phone him as soon as Mike was at sea and we'd arrange when to meet.'

Alvarez imagined the scene. The motor-cruiser casting off with the husband giving a last, fond farewell look at the mountains because near their feet lived his loving wife ... And she was already on the phone, trying to contact her paramour.

She took a small, lace-edged handkerchief from the pocket of her frock and kneaded it with trembling fingers as she said: 'You still haven't told me. Do you think he really has ... has killed himself?'

'Señora, I just cannot say any more than that I have searched the house and the land and have found nothing.' He stood up. 'I will go now and try to discover more.'

'I pray he's safe.' She closed her eyes for a few seconds. 'Will ... will Mike have to know everything?'

'Only if that becomes absolutely necessary, señora. Otherwise I will remain silent,' he said coldly.

He left. There was a hell of a lot to be said for being single.

*

The captain of the Guardia Civil was a large man whose once athletic body was now running to fat. In character an authoritarian, and very aware of the importance of his own position, it irked him beyond measure that Alvarez should work from his post and yet not be directly under his command. He had frequently applied to Palma for Alvarez to be posted elsewhere, but it seemed all his applications must have ended up in wastepaper baskets.

He leaned back in the chair in his ground-floor office and stared across his desk at Alvarez. 'Four men? You want *four* men to search one finca? What's the matter — are you too tired to do it yourself?'

Alvarez answered with the insouciance of a man unplagued by ambition. 'I've searched and there's no sign of him anywhere around the place. But the trees along both sides of the torrente at the bottom of his field go on for a way and he might have strolled some way before he blew his brains out — or maybe he's in one of the fields a bit from the house. He could've reckoned it would be kinder to his wife not to do it in the house or field and so give it a reputation.'

'Where's his wife now?'

'I don't know. I've got to try to find out.'

The captain could think of no valid reason for refusing the request.

*

Alvarez drove down to the Port. He parked under a young palm tree, one of many which lined the sea side, crossed the road, and climbed the rickety wooden stairs to the flat on the first floor. There was a small balcony, then a glass-fronted door. He knocked on the open door, turned, and looked out at the bay. The mountains which ringed it were soft and friendly in outline, the water was azure blue, and the shoreline had not yet been buried under concrete. If only, like some enchanted castle containing the Sleeping Beauty, the bay could stay forever as it was ...

''Morning. What d'you want?'

He turned. The speaker was a man dressed only in a swimming costume. He had a deeply tanned, handsomely built, well muscled body. 'Good morning, señor. I would like, if I may, to speak to Señora Calvin.'

'What about?'

'I would prefer to explain that to her personally.'

'She's busy. In any case, she's not buying anything.' Adamson spoke with careless insolence.

'My name is Inspector Alvarez. Cuerpo de Policia.'

Adamson's expression abruptly changed. 'For Christ's sake, why didn't you say so? I'm sorry, but you didn't ... Come on in and I'll call Brenda.'

At some time or other, thought Alvarez as he stepped into the flat, the man had been in sharpish contact with the Spanish police and had learned to respect their wide powers.

The sitting/dining-room, entered directly from the balcony, was in a complete muddle, with papers and magazines on the floor, the remains of breakfast — perhaps supper as well — on the table to the right of the empty chairs, and a scrumpled frock on one of the shelves of a battered book-case. But Alvarez far preferred this muddle and the dowdy furnishings to the immaculate, expensive interior of the Ormonds' house: this flat spoke of warm, energetic, libidinous life, not deceitful, frigid existence.

Brenda came into the room. She was wearing a T-shirt over a bikini and at first sight could have been wearing nothing under the T-shirt. Alvarez tried to remember when he had last seen anyone so obviously and excitingly lascivious.

He introduced himself and after she was seated, he sat on the second armchair which proved to have broken arms. Adamson pulled one of the dining-room chairs out from under the table and turned it back to front so that he could rest his arms on the top of the back.

Alvarez wondered whether he should present the news of Calvin as good or bad, in view of the fact that Brenda was obviously living with Adamson. Play it safe, he told himself, and keep it neutral. 'Señora, earlier this morning I was called to the finca owned by your husband because it was reported he was missing. There I unfortunately found a note addressed to the police in which he says he has committed suicide.'

She looked at him, amazement elongating her face and making her look as if she had just swallowed something very hot. 'John ... John's killed himself?'

'That is what is written in his note.'

'Oh, my God! ... And has he?'

'I'm sorry, but I cannot answer you. I have searched the house and the land around it and have found nothing. Now I have to have men search the other fields nearby.'

'He'd never commit suicide,' she said with sudden harshness. 'He's a fighter. Anyway, why should he?'

'He was, to my knowledge, in a certain amount of financial trouble.'

'He's always in financial trouble because it hurts him to spend. That would never make him kill himself.'

'This trouble, señora, might have made him spend a very great deal of money.'

'That'd make him choke to death, even if he didn't knock himself off,' said Adamson.

She looked at him, but said nothing.

'Señora, there is a gun cupboard in the study. Were there normally guns in it?'

'There was always one, the one he was so proud of. Isn't … isn't it there now?'

'No, señora.'

'Oh God!'

'There is a message for you, in the note he left in the house. Would you be kind enough to read the note?' He took a brown envelope from his pocket and from it drew out the note he had found in the typewriter. He handed it to her.

She read it through very quickly once, then much more slowly a second time. Tears welled out of her eyes during the second reading: they trickled down her cheek and she shook her head to displace them, as if angrily denying what she read.

'Would you think that is Señor Calvin's signature, señora?'

She nodded, sniffed, then said: 'And it's his way of writing. That sardonic, to-hell-with-you attitude … Oh God! he must have killed himself, then, or he'd never have written such a note and left it.' She looked vaguely at Alvarez, then concentrated her gaze on Adamson. 'Steve, he's dead.'

'Señora,' said Alvarez, 'if I may have the letter back? For the moment I must keep it.'

She handed it to him. 'Steve, he must be dead!'

'You called him enough names when he was alive, so don't get all weepy just because he's turned up his toes.'

'You … you don't understand.'

'Could be.'

'He understood you, right enough. D'you know the last thing he wrote in that letter?'

'How the hell could I, since I haven't read it?'

'He's left me everything, but says to keep it somewhere really safe because I'm too generous with my possessions.'

'Are you saying he's passed the house on to you?'

'That's right.'

'That's great. He wasn't such a complete bastard, after all.'

'Steve! How can you?'

'How can I what?'

'Talk like that about someone who's just dead?'

'Easy.'

'You shouldn't say nasty things about the dead.'

'*De mortuis nil nisi bonum*, and all that? There'll be a hell of a long silence if we try to think of something nice to say about him.'

'You're being quite filthy.' She half turned and spoke to Alvarez. 'He doesn't realize.'

'How much is the house worth?' asked Adamson.

She shrugged her shoulders, then cried a few more tears. 'If I'd still been with him, it wouldn't have happened. I'd have talked him out of it, whatever the trouble was.'

'You'd have been talking yourself out of a house.'

She looked as if about to shout something at him, but finally slumped back in her chair and for a brief moment seemed quite lifeless, like some huge doll carelessly thrown aside.

Adamson spoke to Alvarez, a trace of nervousness in his manner. 'What happens now?'

'Clearly, señor, I have to discover whether Señor Calvin really has committed suicide.'

'It's all a joke,' she said. 'He was always fond of nasty jokes. It has to be one because I can't think of him as dead.'

'Señora, I must go and make further enquiries. If you should learn anything definite, please tell me at the Guardia post in Llueso.'

'And if you learn something definite … come and tell me right away.'

'Of course, señora. Let us hope that since he did make nasty jokes, this is one of them.'

Alvarez said goodbye and then left the room and returned down the rickety steps to the street. He went back to his car and drove along the front road, past a hotel pier which contained a large patio and a swimming pool, and took the next turning to the left which brought him to the square. He parked and went into the corner café and ordered a cognac and a coffee.

'You look kind of harassed,' said the bartender.

'I am. It's been go, go, go, since dawn.'

'You want to watch it. It's that kind of strain which keeps the undertakers rich.'

'And the strain of waiting for what I've ordered.'

The barman chuckled. 'Know something? If you ever need a blood transfusion, they'll have to mix the new blood with cognac or the shock'll be too much for you.'

CHAPTER VIII

The four Guardia Civil were in shirt-sleeves and open necks, but even so they were debilitatingly hot. They sat under the shade of an ancient algarroba tree, whose trunk had been tortured by the centuries, and stared resentfully up at Alvarez.

'You've searched all the nearby fields?'

'Every bloody field this side of Llueso,' said the youngest of the four, who had constituted himself their spokesman.

'And you checked the woods both sides of the torrente?'

'We've been over every square centimetre. And d'you know what it got us?' The guard pulled up his trouser leg to show several scratches.

'We even checked the pigsties down the lane,' said one of the older men, and he laughed.

The youngest Guard turned. 'It's all right for you to snigger! You didn't land in a load of pig muck.'

'Didn't your dad ever tell you it was slippery?'

'When I was a kid I lived in a town where you didn't spend your time paddling in pig muck that stinks.'

'You should've lived forty years ago,' said Alvarez, with all the harsh contempt of a born countryman. 'Then you'd've known a town can stink of worse things than pig muck.'

'Forty years ago you all lived in caves on this bloody island.'

Alvarez was glad he was getting old because he'd discovered he'd nothing at all in common with modern youth: especially modern youth from the Peninsula. He took a pack of cigarettes from his pocket and handed it around and they all smoked.

'He's having you on,' said the youngest Guard resentfully. 'He's no more dead than I am.'

Alvarez scratched his heavy, square chin as he remembered the empty gun cupboard.

'My stomach's telling me it's time to eat,' said one of the other Guards. 'Come on, Enrique, let's call it a day.'

For the moment it was difficult to think what else they could do. After all, if Calvin had shot himself he'd obviously done it at least half a kilometre from his house, and it was virtually impossible to search the rest of the valley which was almost ten kilometres long. Sooner or later the body would turn up. Alvarez stared across the valley at the mountains on the other side and watched a thin coil of smoke rise from the point at which the face became too rocky and sheer for vegetation. 'OK. There doesn't seem anything else we can usefully do, so let's get back and get some grub.'

They came to their feet.

The eldest Guard sniffed loudly. 'I'd say there was a bit of a pong around here somewhere.'

The youngest Guard stamped off out of the shade into the sunshine, to the accompaniment of loud laughter.

'Now what's upset him? No sense of humour — that's the trouble with the youngsters today.'

'They've had it much too easy,' said Alvarez, with companionable agreement.

*

Alvarez cut his siesta very short and left the Guardia post as four o'clock was striking from the church in the square. The heat was greater than ever: it was so hot in the airless street that the sweat poured down his face, neck, back, and chest. Sweet Mary! no man, no matter how great a sinner, should be condemned to work at such a time. If Calvin really had killed himself, then he truly deserved his place in even hotter climes.

He drove out to Ca'n Adeane, to find the maid dusting the sitting-room with plenty of vigour, but little expertise. 'Good afternoon, señora,' he said politely.

She studied him. 'You must be from the police. Is it true? Has the señor cut his throat with a razor that left his head hanging with only one sinew? When I heard, I can tell you I had quite a turn. Can't think of him as dead.'

He crossed to one of the armchairs and gratefully sank down into it.

'Have a seat while we chat.' She was in early middle age, with the tanned, heavily creased face of a woman who had worked for much of her life in the fields. Housework for the foreigner paid far better than endless labouring in the fields, sowing, weeding, and harvesting, by hand, and it did not strain a woman's back and rack her joints in agonizing rheumaticky pains. A few people had reason to be grateful to the foreigners.

She spoke the moment she was seated. The old mother of Juan, the butcher, had told her. Just one piece of sinew left …

'It's not quite like that,' said Alvarez.

She looked disappointed to discover the gory tale was incorrect.

'All we know for certain is he said he was going to commit suicide and now we can't find him: not in the house, the woods, or the fields.'

She sucked in her lower lip, then released it with a plopping noise. 'Then where's he done it?'

'Search me. Maybe he hasn't.'

'If the señor says he's going to do something, he does it. Always has done.'

'I had a word with his wife earlier on — she said it could all be a joke because he'd that sort of a humour.'

'He was always cheerful,' she answered, missing the point of what he'd said.

'D'you know his wife?'

'She was here when I first came to work. Always laughing, but I never knew what about because she can't speak Spanish. We used to talk with hand signals and she got most of them wrong. But she didn't spend all her time running round to see if I was doing the work, like some of the old cows I've worked for.'

'Did she row much with him before they separated?'

'Row? I've never heard better, even though I didn't understand the words.' She chuckled coarsely. 'Thought I was going to see murder done, one day. She threw a shoe at him and missed and knocked over an ornament. Smashed it. You should've seen his face!'

'I suppose you've no idea what they usually rowed about?'

'I didn't need to understand English to know that! Women.'

'He liked 'em?'

'Couldn't keep away from 'em. He's not so young as he was, but you wouldn't know it from the way he carries on. And since his wife cleared out … You wouldn't believe all I could tell you.'

Probably not. He thought how interesting it was the way in which they both switched backwards and forwards from the present to the past when they discussed him. 'How'd you say he's been the last few days?'

'I'll tell you. It's only a day or two ago that I said to myself, there's something serious up and that's fact.'

'Why did you think that?'

'Because he wasn't himself. Snapping, telling me I wasn't doing me job proper — and me keeping the place like a new pin, like always.'

'When did you last see him?'

'It would've been Tuesday afternoon, when I was here.'

'You've just said he was snappy — did he ever suggest he was in some sort of trouble and might do himself in?'

'Never said anything like that.'

'You're being very helpful, señora.'

She smiled complacently. 'I've always kept my ears open.'

'And your eyes, I'll be bound. Tell me — how many guns does he usually have in that cupboard in the end room?'

'One,' she replied immediately. 'But I'm telling you, I'm not allowed to go near the cupboard. "Hands off, not up," he used to say. "That gun's worth more than you are." Come to that, I didn't do the room very often because he didn't seem to want me in there.'

'But you did clean it up from time to time?'

'When he said to.'

'And whenever you've been in there, there's only been the one gun in the cupboard?'

'That's right. One day he took it out and showed it to me. D'you know what he said the gun was worth?'

'I've no idea.'

'A quarter of a million pesetas. He was always joking.'

'This time he was probably not joking. Some English guns are very expensive.'

'But a quarter of a million! Just for a gun what one can buy on this island for ten thousand!' She shook her head and it was obvious she still believed it had been a joke.

'I had a look round this house and noticed the gun cupboard's empty now. Have you seen the gun lying around anywhere?'

'That I haven't, but I ain't done everywhere yet: just the upstairs and a bit of this room here.'

'Let's have a look right round together.' He stood up. 'He might have taken the gun out to clean it and have left it somewhere by mistake.'

But the gun was nowhere in the house.

*

Goldstein drove carefully into the garage and parked with precision, with the windscreen just touching the small plastic marker ball which hung from the ceiling. He switched off the engine and climbed out of the car, closed the garage doors and locked them from the inside, and went through the wash-room into the kitchen. There was the sound of pop music. His lips tightened.

His wife was in the sitting-room, listening to the hi-fi. As he entered, he heard the words: 'Love's a bloom, Or a withered prune: A heart's v-room, Or a maudlin' gloom.' He crossed to the set, pressed the reject switch, and the music ceased. 'God knows how you can listen to such drivel,' he said coldly.

She spoke defensively. 'Not everyone likes Bach.'

'Of course not. Decent music requires a modicum of intelligent understanding before it can be appreciated.'

She looked at him, her expression one of sad resentment. 'Perce, why do you go on and on ... '

'Will you please stop calling me Perce.'

She curled up in the chair, with her bare feet under her, and stared despondently at the carpet.

He walked into the centre of the room and then stopped when six feet from where she sat. He studied her. 'I heard some news just now that's maybe going to interest you.'

She knew, from bitter experience, that such a tone of voice could mean only trouble for herself.

When she didn't answer, he said: 'Have you been out today?'

'You know I haven't, except to go to the shops and buy food.'

'You didn't stop off on the way back and visit some of your strange friends?'

There was usually a point at which she said to herself, 'To hell with it,' and answered him back, even though certain he must inevitably succeed in wounding her far more than she could wound him because he allowed no limits to what he said. 'What's so strange about my friends? They're perfectly normal.'

'That depends on one's definition of normalcy. Is it normal to enjoy a moronic level of life? Or is it normal to demand a level of intelligent sophistication ... '

'For God's sake, put a sock in it.'

'Crudity is the last resort of the mentally bankrupt.'

'Do you know what Hazel said about you the other day?'

'I do not.'

'She said … ' Amanda checked her words. 'Forget it.'

'On the contrary, I wish to know. What did she say?'

'It just doesn't matter.'

'You raised the subject so now you'll complete it. What did she say?'

'That you were so full of wind, it's no wonder you're always gurgling.'

'She is one of the most crude, vapid women I've ever had the misfortune to meet. I'm surprised that even you could find sufficient in common with her to be in the least friendly.'

'She's alive and fun and warm-hearted — not like you. And shall I tell you something? She's got ten times more friends than you: and they're the kind of friends you'd give your right arm to have, but never will, not if you buy two Rolls-Royces and give a thousand quid to every one of Lady Eastmore's pet charities.'

'Your lack of judgement doesn't surprise me.' He crossed to his chair. 'Only that you seem to take pleasure in parading the fact.' He sat down. 'I heard some news this evening, down at the bar, that will interest you.'

She felt frightened because she could see that he believed he was now going to get his revenge for the things she had just said.

'Don't you want to know what the news is? After all, you'll no doubt be rather concerned. Some might say, intimately.'

She had never before heard such hard, vicious anger in his voice.

He was determined to prolong the scene. He leaned across to take a cigar out of the over-ornate silver cigar box which was on the piecrust table near his chair, clipped the end of the cigar with precise, unhurried movements, then struck a match. He drew on the cigar a couple of times, looked at her with eager vindictiveness, finally said: 'The news is about your boy-friend.'

She struggled to retain her composure. 'My what? Percival, please don't be silly and start that up all over again. You know it's terrible nonsense.'

He rolled the cigar between finger and thumb. 'Apparently he's killed himself.'

She sat very still, feeling as if time had ceased. The words went round and round her head, hurting more and more with every repetition.

'He cut his throat from ear to here.' It was typical of him to try to joke when he was mentally hurting her so cruelly.

'No,' she murmured, so quietly that he could not distinguish the words. 'Oh God, no, it can't be true!'

'Bit of a shock to hear he's dead, perhaps? The great love of your life. *Requiescat in pace*, dear John.'

She looked up at him. 'John?'

'Don't, please, insult my intelligence by expecting me to believe your simulated ignorance.'

'Who are you talking about?'

'A man who'll jump into no more beds whilst the husband's away. John Calvin.'

She did the one thing he had not been expecting. She began to laugh.

*

Helen, lying in bed naked because of the heat, heard the car come down the slip road. For a second she knew an increased tension because she thought she didn't recognize the engine note, then she heard the rattle caused by the front suspension: it *was* their Seat. She switched on the bedside light and looked at her watch and saw the time was nearly one o'clock.

The front door slammed shut. 'Jim.' He didn't answer her. Listening to his footsteps, she judged he was crossing to the chest of drinks: a little later there was the clink of glass against glass to confirm her judgement.

He came into the bedroom, a half-empty glass in his right hand. She'd pushed the sheet off herself a long time ago, soon after she'd first tried to get to sleep. She noticed that he did not, for once, look at her naked body with his usual sharp desire. 'Where the hell have you been again?' she demanded.

'Out and about,' he replied. He sat down on the rush-bottomed chair in front of the dressing-table.

'You were out last night until God knows when. Have you any idea what the time is?'

'Not really.'

'When you didn't come back and didn't come back, I was sure you'd had an accident.'

'Getting ready to celebrate?' He drank.

She bit back the sharp answer which immediately came to mind. 'Jim, I'm worried sick. What's been happening? Why are you out so late? Why were you out most of last night?'

'I've just been walking around, trying to work out a plot.'

'Walking in the dark?'

'There's a moon up.'

'For the love of God, stop knocking your brain like this. You can't go on and on.'

'At the moment, I've no option.'

'What's the desperate rush with the book?'

'I'm behind schedule.'

'Whose schedule?'

'My own.'

'Then scrap it. Let's clear out for a week and go to England or France where it's cooler and there'll be a change of scenery.'

He drained his glass. 'My bank balance doesn't allow any trips to anywhere.'

'But mine does.'

'All right. You go to England or France.'

'How many times have I told you that it's not my money, it's ours?' She spoke appealingly. 'Jim, why can't you ease up on your pride and learn to live with and enjoy our money?'

He didn't answer.

'It was all going to be so easy when we got married.'

'Things are notoriously easy then: stardust in the eyes.'

'You were going to pay for the essentials, I was going to pay for the luxuries.'

'Only I was too optimistic. I'd forgotten inflation. Now I can afford to provide either bread or butter, but not both.'

'Then we pool our money and have bread and butter, but no jam.'

'You have your trip to England, I'll stick with dry bread.'

'God, Jim, you're difficult!' she said despondently.

'That's my middle name.' He looked at his glass. 'I'm good for another. What about you?'

She hesitated, then said: 'I'll have a gin and tonic.'

He left. When he returned, he handed her a glass and she sat up to take it. 'Come here, on the bed, Jim.' She patted the bed.

Almost reluctantly, he sat down beside her.

'Relax.'

'I am relaxing.'

She leaned against him, making certain her body pressed hard against his. 'Relax some more.'

For the first time, the set of his mouth lightened. 'Are you sure you know what relaxing means?'

'Didn't you know I'm dead ignorant … Jim, try smiling. It does wonders for your image and makes me want to cuddle you. Forget inflation, publishers, and subscription figures. Laugh and kiss me instead.'

He kissed her. Her free arm tightened around him. He drew back, forcing her to release him.

'Now what the hell's the matter?'

He drank. 'The bar was still open when I came back through the square.'

'Bully for anyone who was thirsty. Now let's forget them and … '

'I saw Vera there.'

She sighed, moved slightly away from him, and sipped her drink. 'So you saw Vera. How tight was she?'

He finished his drink, then looked at the glass as if wondering whether to refill it.

'Have we exhausted the subject of Vera?'

'She told me a rumour that's going the rounds.'

'Who's this one slandering?'

'Helen, you … you're not going to like it. It concerns John. I know what you think of him … '

She broke in, speaking fiercely. 'You don't know a damn thing because you've an imagination ten times too wild. You've convinced yourself I've had an affair with him.'

'Haven't you?' His voice was hoarse. 'You went to his house.'

'And that's proof of adultery? Jim — cool your imagination and stop thinking molehills into mountains. You went on and on about him because I'd talked to him at drink parties we'd been to and it didn't matter how hard I told you he was just someone amusing to talk to, you imagined purple passion. I got bloody sick at you believing I could have an affair just like that. So when he asked me to his place I said yes, out of pique — and also with a bitchy desire to teach him not to count his conquests before he'd bedded them.'

'What happened?'

'I drove to his place and he said how lovely I looked and gave me drinks — enough to make me light-hearted, but not enough to make me careless. Then he served up a meal that would make any cordon bleu jealous.'

'Oysters?'

She laughed.

'He might have tried that old gag.'

'Someone as self-confident as he? Never waste the money.'

'You seem to find it all rather amusing?'

'Good for the ego.'

'So you discovered he was a good cook. Then what?'

'Coffee, liqueurs, and the yawns routine.'

'What the hell's that?'

'Yawn, it's hot, yawn, wouldn't it be more comfortable upstairs, yawn, where it's cooler.'

'What did you say to that?'

'Yawn, I was disappointed, yawn, I'd expected a much more sophisticated approach.'

'You actually said that?'

'Criticize a man's technique and you hit him below the belt. Even Casanova would never have regained the initiative if a lady had told him his kisses were adequate but his tongue-work was poor.'

'How did he react?'

'Badly. He's obviously been spoiled.'

'You didn't go upstairs?'

'Jim!' She put her glass down, took his from his hands and placed it next to hers, then pulled him over and kissed him. She said: 'I suppose I ought to be furious you don't trust me more, but I'll confess I'm rather excited by your stupid jealousy. Pistols at dawn and breakfast for one. Would you challenge him to a duel? I'd never let you actually go and fight him, but I love the idea of being fought over. Does that make me a real bitch?'

He spoke very abruptly. 'What Vera said was, he's killed himself.'

She was silent and motionless for a few seconds, then she said: 'Vera's always talking the most terrible nonsense, especially when she's tight.'

'She swears it's true. Brenda told her.'

'Anything Brenda says is bound to be wrong.'

'The police called at Brenda's place and showed her the note John left in the typewriter. Steve Adamson agrees that happened.'

'Oh!' She held him a shade tighter. 'I ... I still hope it isn't right. Not because there was ever anything between me and John, but because I can't bear to think of anyone killing himself. Anyway, John loves himself much too much to do such a thing.'

'Poor John,' he said suddenly.

'Why d'you say that in that tone of voice?'

'He'd probably no idea how far you saw through him.' She kissed him. Then she ran a fingertip along his cheek. 'Jim, where did you get that bruise?'

'I walked into a branch in the dark.'

'Take a torch next time … Are you satisfied now that I was only a little stupid and didn't do more than play with fire for a short enough time not to get burned?'

'Yes.'

'Yawn, I'm tired. Yawn, wouldn't you be more comfortable lying down?'

'Your technique may be good, but your approach is lousy,' he said, as he undid his shirt and pulled it off.

CHAPTER IX

Alvarez leaned across the desk in his airless office and dragged the Out tray nearer to himself: from it, he took a glass. He pulled open the bottom right-hand drawer of the desk and brought out a bottle of 103 brandy. The bottle was almost empty and he uncharitably wondered if someone had been sneaking in and helping himself, but then decided that that was unlikely. He sighed. He must have drunk more than he'd thought. He poured himself out a large tot.

As he drank, he thought about the finca he'd heard was for sale. Up in the mountains, with a well that was said not to run dry even in the dryest summer; the house was in need of some repair. The terraced land grew olives and a few walnuts. All this for 700,000 pesetas because it was too far away from the coast for any foreigner to be interested in buying it. If he'd had 700,000 pesetas, he'd have bought it the moment he'd heard about it. Modern youth shrank away from the very hard work of harvesting olives, but he knew a deep satisfaction in expertly wielding a seven-metre bamboo to knock olives out of the silver-grey trees, some of which were a thousand years old and looked every one of them.

The telephone rang. He stared at it with dislike as he drank more brandy, but it refused to become silent. Sighing, he lifted the receiver. 'Yeah?'

'Is that Inspector Alvarez? This is Brenda Calvin. Steve said I really must phone you. What I want to know is, is he, or isn't he?'

He scratched his nose with the edge of the glass. 'Is Mr Adamson what?'

'How d'you mean?'

'Señora Calvin, aren't you asking me something about Señor Adamson?'

'Of course not. Why on earth should I? … What I'm asking is, have you found John? It's a whole week now since you came and told me he'd committed suicide …

'I told you only that he had written a note which said he had, señora.'

'That's just the point, isn't it?'

Alvarez began to feel a little out of his depth. 'Señora, do you want to know if I have discovered any proof that Señor Calvin definitely has committed suicide?'

'Thank goodness you've at last understood me.'

'I have to answer, no, señora. I have discovered no such proof.'

'But why not?'

'We have made a second and much wider search, with no result, I have spoken to the bank and no money has been drawn out of his account since a week ago on Monday, I have spoken to friends, none of whom has seen him in the past week. It seems he has vanished, but there is no proof he is dead.'

'Have you spoken to Nancy Ormond?'

'Señora Ormond?' he repeated, speaking as if the name were new to him.

'She was one of his latest. If he hasn't seen her, he's almost certainly dead. Unless, of course, he's found someone else. But I haven't heard any names and people usually rush to tell me. Look, I must know. There's the estate, isn't there?'

If Calvin were provably dead and his will was good — lawyers were checking it now — she inherited the finca and that was worth at least four million pesetas without the contents. Even if she weren't desperately eager to know whether it was legally hers, Adamson would be.

She confirmed his thoughts. 'Steve says you ought to know for sure, one way or the other, by now.'

'Perhaps he would care to suggest what further steps we might take?'

There was a loud, cheerful laugh. 'All he's any good at is criticizing. Isn't it just like him to leave everything up in the air? I'll bet he's laughing his head off, wherever he is.'

A little more in tune with her way of thought, Alvarez was able to judge that the subject of the last two sentences was Calvin, not Adamson.

'Do try and find out for sure. I hate to keep thinking of him in limbo. And apart from anything else, I'm beginning to wonder what I can use for money. My bank manager is really rather a dear, but he just won't let me run up an overdraft, whatever I say. I don't think bank managers out here are as nice as they are in England: I never had any trouble at home getting money. He says it's because out here anyone who lends money is thought a fool for being so weak.'

'Señor Adamson says that?'

'John.'

You couldn't be right every time.

'Do have another look round. If he is waiting to be found, he must be feeling most terribly neglected.' She said goodbye and rang off.

Alvarez finished his drink, then emptied the bottle into the glass. Poor Señor Calvin, so very neglected: like a baritone who'd launched himself into his big aria only to find his audience had cleared off and gone home.

*

After a few days, the disappearance and possible suicide of John Calvin ceased to be the major topic of conversation amongst the English community. From time to time he was still remembered, but mostly people forgot him and discussed the more important things in life, such as the incompetence of the local builders, the deviousness of the local lawyers, the rapaciousness of the local landlords, and the iniquitous way in which gin had gone up to ninety pesetas a litre for a brand that was safe to drink.

Nancy Ormond, however, still mourned him. In fact, she became so listless that her husband took her along to the doctor, who prescribed vitamin pills. These failed to work immediately, so he made her join him on a three-day boat trip to Valencia and back. She was sea-sick throughout the journey and on her return home she retired to bed, totally exhausted.

*

The telephone rang at seven-thirty-three in the morning. Alvarez opened his eyes, stared at the telephone which was dimly visible in the very subdued light, and gloomily wondered why things were always happening on a Sunday. He reached out and lifted up the receiver. 'What is it?'

'This is the Guardia post, Inspector. Earlier this morning, at seven-twenty-five, we received an important communication.'

Sweet Mary! thought Alvarez. Who could be making this text-book report? 'All right. Now let's hear what the earth-shattering communication is all about.'

'The body of a deceased man has been discovered on the upper slopes of Puig Pamir.'

'And where in the hell's Puig Pamir?'

'It is to the west of the Llueso/Laraix road, Inspector Alvarez, and it attains a height of nine hundred and sixty-two metres.'

'Fascinating! And what has the body attained?'

'A somewhat damaged condition, according to the report.'

'Who found it?'

'A shepherd, searching for a sheep missing from his flock … '

'Where will I find the shepherd?'

'At Ca'n Pequeño. We have ascertained where that is and it is very close to Ca'n Adeane, which is the house belonging to the missing Englishman. Clearly one should not speculate at this juncture … '

'You speculate all you like. I'll get along there.'

He washed and shaved, dressed, and went along to the kitchen. His nephew (the relationship was more distant, but by tradition he was called Uncle) was rooting about in the refrigerator. 'Is there anything good to eat?' asked Alvarez.

'There's some negro, but Mummy said I mustn't have any now. Would you like some? It smells delicious. I'm sure you'd like it.'

'No, thanks,' he replied, knowing perfectly well what were his nephew's true motives. In his estimation, all children were natural criminals at heart and education consisted in suppressing those criminal instincts in so far as this was possible.

'There's nothing else worth eating,' said his nephew, in tones of disgust. 'Only some mucky soup.'

'Just what I wanted. A bowlful inside me and maybe I'll feel slightly more human.'

'Wouldn't you feel better if you didn't drink so much cognac? Why do you drink so much, Uncle?'

'You are being impossibly rude. In any case, I don't know the answer.'

The boy laughed, then brought out from the refrigerator a plastic jar half full of soup. He asked Alvarez how much he wanted, poured some of the soup into a saucepan and put this on the gas.

Alvarez had two thick slices of bread with the soup, a cup of instant coffee and a small brandy afterwards, and then, when he'd smoked the cigarette, he left.

Ca'n Pequeño, true to its name, was very small. To some eyes it was probably also mean in character, but Alvarez saw it as an attractive house because it was unchanged after a couple of hundred years and had not been bought by a foreigner and modernized.

The shepherd was a small man, with a face puckered by age and tanned by the weather. He walked with bowed back and a shuffling gait, as if every movement were an effort, yet he covered the ground with surprising speed, talking continuously and clearly suffering from no shortage of wind. They went up a dirt path which led off at right angles from the dirt track and this soon began to wind its way up the side of the mountain. Alvarez struggled along behind the shepherd for as long as he could, but when the gap between them became too great and his lungs were giving him hell, he called a halt. He took a handkerchief from his pocket and mopped his sweating face and neck. 'How ever much further is there to climb?'

The shepherd laughed mockingly. 'You're not in any condition, are you?'

'It's a Sunday.'

'Wouldn't make any difference if it was Monday. You're too fat. You young 'uns are all the same: eat and drink too much.'

'And the old 'uns talk too much ... How much further is the stiff?'

'Up a bit yet. Think you'll make it?'

Alvarez mopped his face again, returned the handkerchief to his pocket. He sighed heavily, then forced his leaden feet onwards. The path wound its way between boulders and outcrops of rock and seemed to become steeper with every metre.

The shepherd stopped and turned. 'I'll tell you something. If I'd of known you weren't fit, I'd've said come up the other way by car.' He laughed shrilly.

'Are you bloody telling me there's a car track we could've taken?'

'Never crossed me mind 'til now when I saw you panting and sweating like a man near to quittin'.'

Alvarez swore, yet within him there was a thin shaft of reluctant amusement: the Mallorquin peasant always had been a great man for slyly knocking authority. The shepherd would enjoy himself for days remembering all the physical discomfort he had caused the detective.

They resumed their march and finally reached the end of the path, immediately above which was a natural shelf, formed when a huge mass of rock had broken off at some time in the distant past.

The body, slumped sideways, lay against the sheer face of rock which backed the shelf. 'Ain't too pretty to look at,' said the shepherd, with relish. It was a gross understatement. Even Alvarez, who had met brutal death before, swallowed heavily when he first studied the body. The gun had originally made a mess of part of the head and the heat and the flies had carried on from there.

The shepherd pointed. 'It's a lovely gun he used: never seen one like it before.'

'D'you touch it?'

'I ain't that soft ... What d'you reckon'll happen to it?'

'I wouldn't know, except it won't finish up in your thieving hands.' Alvarez walked up to the body. Why did death so often have to be degrading? Man was mortal, but there should have been other ways of proving it than to let a body become host to maggots.

'I suppose it's that silly bugger of an Englishman?' said the shepherd. 'Was he a millionaire?'

'Probably only if you count in other people's money.' Alvarez hunkered down and stared at the gun. The butt had been between the feet when it was fired and there was a small 'star' on the rock, hammered out when the gun recoiled. Because it was difficult — though not impossible — to put the muzzles of a normally barrelled twelve bore in one's mouth and then pull a trigger with a forefinger, string had been looped from the for'd trigger, round the butt, and back up. The end of this string lay near the left hand. After the explosion the body had keeled over from its sitting position and the gun had been pushed sideways so that now it stuck out at an angle and was aimed well to the left.

Alvarez gripped the gun by the muzzles — very slightly tarnished by rust — and pulled it free. He pressed the locking bar, but applied no pressure to the barrels: the gun opened to show it was self-opening. The right-hand cartridge had been fired, the left-hand one hadn't: strangely, the fired cartridge was not ejected when the gun broke. Faulty ejector, he thought, gratified to discover that even the best products of England were no longer free from faults. He raised the breech above the butt and the two cartridges fell into the palm of his left hand. He closed the gun, briefly examined the chasing which proved to be of superb quality, dropped the cartridges into his trouser pocket, then tried the gun for balance and brought it to his shoulder.

'What's it like?' asked the shepherd eagerly.

'As if it were part of me.'

'Let's have a go with it.'

Alvarez lowered the gun. 'All right. But you drop it, or put the smallest of dents in the barrels, and I'll have you locked up until you're ten years dead and buried.' He passed the gun over.

The shepherd raised it and swung on to a soaring swallow which skimmed the rock face. When the swallow disappeared behind an outcrop, he lowered the gun. 'If I'd of had one like this when I was younger, I'd've kept my family just by shooting. If it ever comes up for sale, let us know, will you?' Very reluctantly, he passed it back.

'Sure.' Alvarez hadn't the heart to destroy a daydream by telling him that the gun would cost much more than his flock of sheep was worth. He carefully laid the gun down on the rock, triggers uppermost.

He examined the body. The shirt, monogrammed J.C., was — where it wasn't stained — light puce and obviously of very good quality: the linen trousers were dark blue: the brown sandals were locally made and expensive. He checked the contents of the trouser pockets: a ring of keys, probably car keys, and a handkerchief monogrammed J.C.

Examined close to, the damage to the head was even more terrible and Alvarez swallowed heavily more than once: his feelings were not improved by the fact that the shepherd clearly felt no such revulsion. The column of shot had pulverized much of the face above the mouth and on the rock, at a height slightly above that at which the head would have been when the body was in a sitting position, were several stains.

He stood up and looked out across the valley. He looked at the fields and trees in their many different shades of green, the scattered houses, the range of mountains with the deep blue sky above them to highlight their jagged crests, and he thought that if a man wanted to fill his soul with beauty in an attempt to justify his existence just before he ended it, nowhere in the world could better serve him than this rocky ledge along the Laraix valley.

'He's messed up my day right proper, he has,' said the shepherd. 'All this time wasted, bringing you up here. What's more, I've still that bloody sheep to find.'

Alvarez continued to look out across the valley. 'How d'you come to lose one — forget to hobble it?'

'What d'you take me for? Me forget to hobble a sheep? I've been minding sheep since I was a nipper.'

Alvarez ceased to listen. When a man committed suicide with a shotgun, what were his last thoughts before he pulled the trigger? Did he wonder at the chain of events which had defeated his pride? Did he stand aside from himself, look down at the crouching figure with the gun muzzles in his mouth, and pity what he saw? Or did he hate what he saw? Or did he just say, 'What the hell?' and pull the string, hoping that everything happened too quickly for him to feel the column of shot tearing his flesh apart …

*

The garage of Ca'n Adeane was to the left and behind the house, in the direction of the woods which bordered the torrente. It was built of breeze blocks which had been plastered over and rising damp had stained the sides brown to a height of a metre. The two wooden doors had been newly painted a light shade of green.

Alvarez tried the Yale-type key from the bunch of keys taken from the pocket of the dead man and it turned the tumblers of the lock. Inside was a Peugeot 504, left-hand drive, on English plates. The law regarding tourist and foreign-plated cars owned by residents had been altered, but Calvin had not been the kind of man to worry about such things as that.

He climbed into the car and sat behind the wheel. He tried the ignition key and it fitted. He started the engine, ran it for a few seconds, then switched off and withdrew the key.

He went into the house — the maid had shown him where the front-door key was kept under a flowerpot — and upstairs to the large bedroom. In the built-in cupboard which covered the whole of one wall was a shoe rack. The shoes on this rack were size forty-five and that was the size of the sandals on the body.

*

Brenda Calvin had the kind of body which theoretically should never have been squeezed into a bikini, but somehow with her the abundance of flesh which overflowed the small scraps of material was, in male eyes at least, sensually attractive, not vaguely obscene. She lay on her stomach on a towel with her bikini top undone, letting the burning sunshine envelop her.

'Señora Calvin.'

She opened her eyes. 'Who's that and what's the panic?'

'Inspector Alvarez, señora. I would like a word with you, if I may?'

She rolled over, only remembering at the very last minute to grab at her bikini top and press it down. 'Oops! Nearly lost it that time.'

Alvarez looked along the beach and tried in his mind not to fill in the shapes he had so nearly seen.

She tied the bikini top behind herself. 'What's brought you here?' She studied his face and drew in her breath. 'Have ... have you found him?'

'Yes, señora,' he answered quietly.

'And he's dead?'

'I am very sorry. Yes, he is dead. Perhaps we can go to your flat?'

She stood up, picked up the towel, turned to face the road, then turned back. 'I know it's silly of me, but I've been hoping terribly he was alive and just having a joke on us all. It's not that emotionally he still means anything much to me ... At least, I didn't think he did ... ' She stopped as she brushed some sand from her golden midriff and Alvarez watched her hands and wondered if her flesh felt as honey smooth as it looked.

'Did John shoot himself?' she asked.

'Yes, he did.'

'That bloody gun! Guns have always scared me silly. But he used to go shooting a lot in England and although he wasn't a man to boast in that sort of a way, he always said he was a really good shot. He certainly loved that gun. I've seen him take ages and ages cleaning it and rubbing it down with an oily rag as if it were going to purr. Was he ... badly hurt?'

'Señora, I have to tell you that a shotgun is very destructive.'

She moved abruptly and crossed the short stretch of sand to the pavement, where she waited under the shade of a palm tree. When the road was clear, she crossed. She climbed the rickety wooden stairs to her flat.

Adamson was sprawled out in one of the battered armchairs. He wore only pyjama trousers, he hadn't shaved, and he was noticeably bleary-eyed. He stared at Alvarez with an obsequious dislike, cleared his throat noisily, then said as belligerently as he dared: 'What's got you back? Have you turned up the old bastard?'

'Don't talk like that, Steve,' she said unhappily.

'I'm not going to shed crocodile tears — and there's no call for you to do so, considering what you used to call him. A man doesn't become a saint just because he's dead.' He turned towards Alvarez. 'Isn't that right?'

'He doesn't become one without dying ... Señora, I am very sorry but there has to be an identification and you will have to make it. It cannot be pleasant, but please understand I will do my best to make it as little unpleasant as possible.'

She shivered, then reached out for the nearest chair and sat down. Her voice shook. 'I can't stand death. It terrifies me. John used to laugh at me because of it and tell me death was the only certain thing in life, but he couldn't understand. I need to believe I'll go on living for ever and ever but when I meet death I know I can't ... '

'Señora, I also am the same. Probably, underneath, we all are. Maybe the kindest thing we can do for ourselves is to pray for a death which comes up from behind and blinds us before we know it's there.'

Adamson laughed. 'Today's funny story.'

'You bloody fool!' she shouted.

He looked angrily bewildered.

She slowly stood up. 'Will you help me?'

'Of course,' said Alvarez. 'As I have told you, I will do all I can.'

'Here,' said Adamson, 'if that's the way you feel, Boo, I'll chuck a few clothes on and come along and hold your hand.'

'Get lost,' she snapped.

*

The morgue was at the back of the undertakers, on the ground floor. There was no sign to show what the building housed, but the road outside was the only one in the town in which the children never played.

Alvarez led Brenda into the waiting-room, barely furnished with only three wood and rush seats, a small table with a vase of cut flowers on it, two framed texts from the Bible, and a painting of the Virgin Mary. The undertaker was as broadly built as Alvarez, with the ruddy complexion and the deliberate movements of a man of the fields, but he also had a natural dignified grace and his manner was without the slightest trace of professional sanctimoniousness. He greeted Brenda in English, then said to Alvarez in Mallorquin: 'Has someone warned her?'

'I have. But let's keep it as low key as we possibly can. She's in a bit of a state.'

'Of course.'

They entered the mortuary, newly equipped with a freezing compartment which contained two cabinets. The undertaker rolled out one of the compartments and pulled back the white shroud, leaving just the head covered. Belinda grabbed hold of Alvarez's arm and squeezed it hard.

'They're his,' she said in a strained whisper. 'He was wearing those clothes the last time I saw him.'

'Did he ever have on any kind of personal jewellery?'

'He … he always wore a signet ring which I gave him when we got married. He wore it even after we'd separated. He used to say … ' She stopped.

Alvarez gently released his arm, went over to the compartment, lifted the right hand, and eased off the gold signet ring from the middle finger. He handed it to her.

She began to cry as she said: 'They're our two initials, J and B. I had them entwined. For a long time, I thought that their being entwined really meant something.'

The undertaker pulled the shroud back over the body and rolled the compartment into the cabinet.

Alvarez guided Brenda out into the hot sunshine.

CHAPTER X

Mallorquins were as great traditionalists as the Spaniards — only the law ever made the mistake of calling the islanders Spaniards — and the square was still the focal point, even the *raison d'être*, of every village. In Llueso, the post office, the telegraph office, the Guardia post, the municipal police post, were just off the square, whilst in it the vegetable and fish market was held every Sunday morning, all fiestas started or finished there, proclamations were proclaimed there, dogs were injected against rabies there ... and at any hour of the day and most of the hours of the night, Mallorquins and foreigners sat at the outside tables of the two cafés which immediately bordered the raised half of the square — designed to give a level surface on a sloping site — and they drank and watched the world go by.

Meegan stirred his coffee. He nodded briefly at a couple who strolled towards his table, then busied himself in lighting a cigarette before they could take his greeting as an invitation to sit down and talk. A very faint breeze stirred the leaves of the plane trees which ringed the square and somewhere nearby, but out of sight, a group of children began to sing and by some near miracle they were all in tune.

Helen came round the side of the church and past the small enclosed fish market with its stone benches and he knew a sudden sharp mental pain because in his eyes she was so beautiful. She saw where he was seated and crossed the square. 'Poor Mary — she was bad tonight.' Once a week, usually on a Sunday evening, she visited an elderly and crippled English woman who lived on her own because she had been deserted by her husband who could not bear her continuing incapacity. Helen sat. 'She was in terrible pain.'

'I wonder why she doesn't go home?'

Helen shrugged her shoulders. It was not a question anyone other than Mary could answer and she never spoke about her personal life.

'What are you going to have to drink?' he asked.

'Just coffee, thanks. Mary gave me an enormous brandy.'

He raised his hand to catch the attention of a waiter.

'By the way, she's heard from someone that the police have finally found John, dead.'

He swung round, dropping his arm and catching his glass to knock it to the ground where it smashed.

She stared at him, her expression strained. 'What ... what in God's name is the matter?'

He struggled to speak calmly. 'It's just I was surprised and forgot the glass was there.' The couple at the next table were staring at him: he showed them in pantomime how the glass had come to be broken and they smiled.

She leaned forward and put her hand on his right arm, which rested on the table. 'Jim, what's the matter? What's worrying you sick?'

'Nothing is.'

'You looked as if something had frightened you into next week.'

'I told you. I was just surprised.'

'Why? You knew he'd said he'd committed suicide.'

The waiter came over and Meegan explained what had happened with the glass. 'No worry,' said the waiter, in heavily accented English. He brushed the bits of glass together with his shoe, said he'd sweep them up later, took their order, and left.

Meegan brought out a pack of cigarettes from his pocket. 'What else had Mary heard about John?'

She shook her head. 'Nothing more.'

A couple, nicknamed the biggest boars in Spain, came up the wide steps on to the level section, looked round, saw Helen and Meegan, and crossed. 'Hullo, there,' said the man. 'Long time, no see. In fact I was only saying to the little lady wife yesterday that it was simply months and months since we'd seen Helen and Jim ... Don't mind if we join you? Lovely evening, isn't it? And it's raining back home. Talk about laugh! Us here, sitting out for a snifter, all of 'em back home huddling in their houses ... Have you heard the news?'

'About poor John? Yes,' said Helen.

'D'you know, he'd put the muzzle of the gun in his mouth and pulled the triggers! Half his head was missing. Just think of it! Half his head.'

Meegan's voice was high. 'You mean ...' He stopped abruptly.

'I'll tell you something. I wouldn't want to eat a plateful of Frito Mallorquin after seeing him, that I wouldn't.'

'Arthur!' said his wife, with the delighted indignation of a woman stupid enough to be amused by her husband's repeated gaucheries.

The waiter came to the table with two coffees. The man said in a loud, hectoring voice: 'I'll have a large gin and tonic and the little lady wife'll have the same.' He repeated the order, even more loudly, although it was obvious the waiter had understood, then turned back. 'I'll tell you something more. There's going to be no end of trouble over his having committed suicide. At the best of times, us English get buried well away from all true believers — all on account of 'Enery the Smart.'

'Who?' asked his wife dutifully.

''Enery the Eighth. Six wives and never paid a halfpenny in alimony — you can't get smarter than that.' He roared with laughter. 'So like I was saying, what are they going to do with the body? There'll be no cemetery that'll have him.'

Meegan stubbed out his cigarette. 'D'you think John would give a damn where he was buried?' He drank his coffee.

'No knowing, is there? I met a bloke who was always going on and on about how death was toes up and that's it. Then he turned up his toes. Guess what? In his will there were orders for a slap-up funeral and a tombstone big enough to live under — or die under, eh? Know what I call that? Buying the insurance too late! ... Been busy writing, then? Churning 'em out? Didn't win the Nobel prize for literature last year, I see. But I'll have a quid on you for this year. Not that I've ever read one of your books — can't really find what I like out here.'

'They do have English comics down at the Port.'

He stared at Meegan, his round, turkey-cock face expressing perplexity. Then he decided to accept it as a joke. 'That's a good one, that is. Very comical — what?'

Meegan saw Helen had finished her coffee. He stood up. 'We've got to go.'

Helen tried to make their departure seem less abrupt. 'I've left something cooking in the oven.'

'Not a bun?' said the man, and laughed again.

Helen ignored him. 'And you know what the man in the house is like if his food is even slightly dried out or burned?'

The woman sniffed. 'Anyone moans about the food I serve up, I tells 'em, cook it yourself. I never have stood any nonsense in my kitchen and that's fact, as Arthur'll tell you.'

'That's fact,' said her husband. 'I can remember when she was preparing a five quid special — that's a tart. Got it? — and I went into the kitchen ... '

Meegan turned and walked into the café where he paid for the two coffees. When he returned outside, Helen joined him. They crossed to the steps, went down them and along to where their car was parked.

When they were both seated, she said: 'Did you have to be quite so rude?'

'In words of one syllable, yes.' He engaged the starter and the engine fired, then died. The same thing happened a second time and he swore with rough violence.

'Try accelerating as soon as it fires,' she suggested.

'Try a seven-pound hammer. The only way you can ever keep a car running on this bloody island is never take it to a garage. The last time it was in for service ...'

'Jim, don't get like some of the English who criticize everything and everybody, but still go on living here.'

'In our case ... '

'In our case, we're here because it's so much better for my health. And until recently, we've both liked living here, despite the mañanas. But ... ' She looked briefly at him. 'But since you got that bee in your bonnet about John you've been a different person: bitter about so many things.'

'With cause.'

She didn't try to argue further.

He started the car and this time kept the engine running, backed, turned, and went down a one-way street and out to the Palma/Puerto Llueso road. He was silent for the seven-minute drive to their house and she made no effort to break that silence, but as soon as they were both indoors she faced him. Her expression was troubled and fearful. 'Jim, please tell me now we're on our own. What is the matter?'

'Nothing. I keep telling you that. Try changing the record.' He went over to the settee and slumped down on it.

'Something is worrying you sick.'

'I'm no more worried than usual when my book won't ... '

'Whatever it is, it's nothing to do with your book.'

'If you know all the answers, stop asking the questions.'

She nibbled her lower lip, somehow managing to contain her normally volatile temper. 'It's to do with John, isn't it? When I told you the police had found his body, you were frightened. Why? You knew he'd said he was going to kill himself.'

'I didn't believe he'd ever really do it.'

'If that were the case, you'd have been surprised, not frightened.'

'You're imagining how I felt.'

'And did I imagine the way you knocked that glass off the table or your shocking rudeness to Arthur?'

'He's so thick-skinned he'll have thought I was being polite.'

She crossed to the settee and sat down beside him. 'Why won't you tell me, so I can help?'

'There's nothing to help over.' He stood up. 'D'you want a drink?'

'I'd like that seven-pound hammer you were talking about earlier,' she said, her voice bitter and strained.

*

Alvarez usually spent Sunday evenings at the Club Llueso. There, he would lose a few pesetas at the local variety of two-handed whist, at which he was a poor player, drink too many brandies, and smoke too many cigarettes. His cousin's family would have been happy if he'd spent the evenings with them, but he was determined to remain as independent as he could: one day they might no longer be able to have him live with them and then he didn't want the hurt of loneliness to be too great.

Pedro slapped down the two of trumps to take the last trick. 'Got you again, Enrique. That's another twenty pesetas.'

'If only I could catch you actually palming the cards.' He took a handful of loose change from his pocket and counted out twenty pesetas. 'There you are — add that to your fortune. Next thing is, you'll get a stroke from too much luxurious living.'

'Or women,' said Pedro slyly. Since he was nearly seventy, there was cause for his amusement. 'By the way, d'you hear about Juan, the baker?'

'What's he been up to this time?'

'Working too hard. The stupid simpleton has been baking bread and cakes so hard he's never stopped to wonder what Marie was really doing when she told him she was working down in the Port two days a week for a Frenchman. Now the Frenchman's returned to France and she's gone with him. And taken all the thousand peseta notes he'd tucked away in their mattress.'

'More fool him for leaving the money where a woman could get at it.' He called across to the barman for two more brandies.

A man walked up to where they sat, by one of the windows, and he shouted at the barman, 'Make that three.' He sat down at the table. 'D'you hear about poor old Juan? His wife's gone off to Italy with an Italian.'

'France, with a Frenchman,' corrected Pedro.

'I'm telling you, it was an Italian.'

'And I'm telling you … '

'Keep your blood pressures low and forget it,' cut in Alvarez. 'Ten to one she's at home right now. And tomorrow she'll be in the shop, trying to overcharge us all as usual.'

The waiter brought three brandies to the table and Pedro went to pay him, but Alvarez said: 'This round's on me.'

'It's what? You lose a fortune and then offer to pay for a round without me reminding you it's your turn. What's up? Have you won the lottery?'

'I just feel good. All my major troubles are behind me, I haven't a wife to take off with a Frenchman, or an Italian, and I'm one day nearer retirement than I was yesterday.'

Fernadez — the newcomer — produced a pack of cigarettes and offered them. As he flicked open a lighter, he said: 'Someone was telling me that the Englishman who blew his brains out used a gun worth a king's ransom.'

'I've handled some guns in my time,' said Alvarez, 'but that one was something different. It sits in your hand like a feather and it comes up to your shoulder like it was doing it on its own.'

'A gun like that must cost something?'

'A quarter of a million, so the Englishman once said.'

Fernadez whistled. Pedro said: 'If it'd been me, I'd've sold it for the quarter million, spent the money on fun, and then blown my brains out.'

Fernadez spoke sarcastically. 'What with, if you'd sold the gun?'

'Someone else's I'd borrowed. Don't ask bloody silly questions.'

'It'll probably go to his wife,' said Alvarez. 'Now she can sell it and have the fun.'

'More fool him. Leave a wife too much and there's a smart fancy-pants knocking at the front door before your coffin's had time to settle.'

'If that's how you feel, don't marry.'

'And get like you?' Pedro laughed shrilly. 'By God! I'd rather marry a real witch and take the consequences.'

Alvarez drained his glass and then looked up at the clock on the wall behind the bar. 'I'll be on my way — I've a hell of a day tomorrow, coping with all the bumf over the Englishman. God knows why he couldn't have knocked himself off in the next department ... Ah, well, life's never perfect!'

He left the club and walked along the narrow roads which were without pavements — up to four years before they had been only packed earth and stone. It was almost dark and the well separated street lights were switched on, casting long shadows across the shuttered houses. At night time — when youngsters weren't tearing the place apart on their motorbikes — there was a peace about the place which soothed a man's soul, even a man of the soil who basically disliked all villages. Perhaps, he thought, it was because within the area in which he lived almost all the houses were old: when a man reached a certain age, there was something very comforting in the past.

His cousin and her husband were in the sitting-room watching the television, now much clearer since a new repeater station had been built on a hill near Puig Llueso: before then the repeater had been on Puig Llueso and the reception had not only been poor, but the nuns had switched off the repeater whenever they considered the subject-matter was in danger of becoming of doubtful morality. His cousin asked him to join them, but he thanked her, said he was too tired, and went upstairs, thinking as he did so that that last brandy had been the dangerous one.

In bed, he tried to read, but the lines of print became too mobile — thanks to that last brandy — and so he switched off the light and prepared to sleep. Immediately, his mind became uneasily active.

Was suicide the act of a coward or a brave man? It was interesting that Calvin had chosen to kill himself up on that rock shelf so that he could take a last look at the starkly beautiful mountains and lush green valley, only lightly brushed by man's work — a final assurance that although his life was about to end, life went meaningfully on. Death could teach more than life. Even Calvin's sardonic, iconoclastic nature had bowed before the teachings of death.

What a gun! When he'd been young he'd gone shooting with a gun which should have exploded in his face whenever he fired it, but mercifully hadn't. He was now saddened to remember that the ejector had been broken, because when he handled something so superbly made he felt offended, disillusioned, when it proved to be faulty ... A hammerless ejector, he suddenly thought, ejected only when the chamber had just been fired: breaking the gun and then closing it again re-cocked it so that when it was next broken without being fired, it would not eject.

He silently swore. That bloody last cognac.

CHAPTER XI

The sunshine which filtered through the louvres of the shutters was reflected off the highly polished dressing-table on to the ceiling in blobs of light which danced. Watching them, Alvarez was reminded of a dance he had gone to with Juana-Maria, when for the first time he had dared to hold her tightly to himself even though her duenna had been sitting very upright on a wooden bench against one of the walls. Duennas! What would the modern youngster, chewing gum, pockets filled with pesetas, sophisticatedly certain the world owed him a living, say if his girl-friend came with her duenna?

Any mechanical thing could go wrong, then right itself for no apparent reason. Was there a television owner who hadn't suffered a fault which never repeated itself when the repairman arrived? If the Purdey now ejected every single time it was fired, this wouldn't *prove* that it had been opened by someone after it had fired the fatal shot ... Yet the odds must surely be ...

He looked at his watch. In ten minutes' time, he must get up. His indecision made him swear. Forget the cartridge which hadn't been ejected and the case was over and done with, bar the paperwork. But start asking questions, questions which could surely only have initially occurred to a mind awash with brandy, and there was no knowing where it would all end ...

He slept wearing only a pyjama bottom. He sat upright and put his feet on the tiled floor. For a while his head pounded, but then it eased off sufficiently for him to consider moving further. A happy man was a wise man (who didn't drink too much) and a wise man always tried to find the easiest possible passage through life. He would forget the Purdey which had once not ejected and he would write his report to Palma, saying he had carried out his investigations and Señor Calvin had committed suicide by blowing half his head off.

*

The Guardia post in Llueso was in an old building which was in urgent need of renovation — a new post, with quarters for married families, was being built down in the Port — and cockroaches were a frequent fact of life. Alvarez had a primitive, illogical, and unthinking fear of them. He leapt back as a black shape scuttled away from the bicycle which had just been moved.

The Guard who was in charge of the exhibits room roared with laughter. 'Run, man, or he'll have your guts for garters.'

'Bloody things,' muttered Alvarez.

'They're deadly, right enough. I knew a bloke who fell asleep in his office and when he woke up they'd eaten shoes, socks, and all the flesh on his feet and he was looking at his own bones.'

'So they transferred him to the skeleton staff ... Come on, cut the cackle and reach over for that gun.'

'All right, all right. There's no need to get sharp. Or are you going shooting? Bring us back a plump partridge if you are.'

'At this time of the year? Give over.'

The Guard handed Alvarez the shotgun. He began to walk towards the door.

'Hang on, mate. You've got to sign it out.'

'What the hell for? I only want it for a few minutes.'

'You know the rules, Enrique.'

'Feed 'em to the cockroaches.'

He went up the stairs to his office, put the gun on the desk, sat down, and looked at it. There was dried blood on the muzzles, looking more like old varnish, and an overall light haze of rust which had been caused by the dew over successive nights up on the rock shelf. Instinctively, he wanted to get an oily rag and remove as much of the rust as possible.

He opened the top right-hand desk drawer and brought out the two cartridges which had been in the gun. He placed them, brass caps downwards, on the desk alongside the trigger guard and then put on his glasses which he needed more often than he used them. He examined the cartridge which had been fired and found on the edge of the brass cap a small mark which suggested it had struck something hard — rock?

He removed his spectacles, took from his pocket two used cartridges he had brought with him, picked up the gun and inserted them in the chambers. He slid the safety-catch forward with his thumb and pulled the front trigger: there was the sharp metallic sound of the firing pin striking the cap. He broke the gun and the right-hand cartridge was ejected in an arc which took it high over his shoulder. He 'fired' the right-hand barrel a dozen times and a dozen times the cartridge was ejected.

He replaced the gun on top of the desk and sat down. As he'd told himself earlier that morning, the fact that he couldn't now get the gun to malfunction did not prove that it had not malfunctioned the previous month. But it did mean that he had now to accept the possibility that when he'd picked up the gun on the rock ledge and broken it, the fired cartridge had not been ejected because the gun had been broken after the fatal shot had been fired.

*

The shepherd, looking if anything a little older and a little more gnarled, was by the edge of the road, leaning on a stick and watching both a flock of sheep and lambs which were grazing the verge and his black and white bitch.

Alvarez braked his car to a halt and climbed out. 'Did you find the missing sheep?'

'Aye. The silly sod'd got itself tied up in some brambles.' The shepherd hawked and spat. 'There's only one thing dafter than sheep. Humans.'

'They're a nice even flock.'

'They should be, seein' as they've all been bred by me.'

'Really sound hindquarters.'

'Reckon to know something about 'em?'

'I should do. I was born on a farm.'

'Was you now?' The shepherd studied Alvarez. 'I allows I thought you wasn't the usual daft bugger of a policeman what doesn't know a ewe from a teg. Not that you aren't too fat around the guts.'

'Dieting is dangerous at my age.' Alvarez took a pack of cigarettes from his pocket. 'D'you use these things?'

The shepherd helped himself and then waited for a light. One of the sheep approached to within half a metre of the road and he clicked his fingers: immediately, the dog ran forward to drive the sheep further back.

Alvarez struck a match. A car went past at high speed, leaving behind a trail of dust which took a time to settle. 'Always rushing,' said the shepherd, with contempt. 'Them's rushing here, t'others rushing there. What's it get 'em?'

'Ulcers.' Alvarez moved into the shade of an evergreen oak and smoked. Because he was from peasant stock, he could understand another peasant. If he baldly tackled the shepherd about the gun, he would either be told a lie or be refused any answer. If he waited, showing endless patience, he would probably learn the truth.

The shepherd took off the dirty straw hat he was wearing and fanned his face with it. 'It's warming up some.' He replaced the hat.

'It's that, all right.'

'Been a dry year, except for that storm.'

'They say the wells are failing. The trouble is, too many people after the water now, with all the tourists.'

'Them! Killed one of me lambs a year or two back. The car didn't stop and I weren't able to get its number.' The shepherd smoked. When the cigarette was finished, he dropped the butt on to the road and carefully stamped it out. 'Come to ask me something, have you?'

'That's right.'

'Well I ain't heard what it is, yet?'

Alvarez shrugged his shoulders. Then, as if it were a reluctant afterthought, he said: 'D'you remember the gun?'

'Ain't likely to forget that.'

'Tell me something. Before I got there with you ... Near killed me that climb did! Took me hours to recover.'

The shepherd laughed shrilly.

'When you first found the stiff, did you pick up the gun and have a feel of it and see what it'd be like for shooting?'

'I told you, didn't I? I ain't soft. You could've been one of those smart buggers from the Peninsula and if I'd so much as touched it, you'd've said I was after pinching it.'

'Fair enough. Looks like, then, I've got to take your finger-prints.'

'I said I never touched it and ... '

'There's no call for worry. I handled it and you had a swing with it and back at the post a Guard touched it. If I take the prints of the three of us and of the dead man and check 'em against the prints on the gun I'll see if someone else had a go with it.'

For the first time, the shepherd looked at Alvarez with respect. 'Just like the telly, that's what!'

*

Alvarez was not very expert at taking fingerprints and by the time he had obtained a reasonable set of the dead man's, he was freely cursing all modern aids to crime detection. He packed the small plastic case, thanked the undertaker for his help, and returned to the Guard post.

Up in his office, he painted light aluminium powder over all parts of the gun. There were prints on the firing holds — the fore part of the barrels and the stock below the trigger guard — and one just on its own. Surely Calvin hadn't carried it by its firing points all the way up to the ledge? Could he have wiped it clean as a symbolic act before shooting himself? Too far-fetched? Or had someone else wiped it clean to try and erase his own prints just in case the staged suicide began to break down?

He examined and compared the few prints which had not been overlaid and smudged beyond any chance of identification. He found one print of the shepherd's, two of his own, and one which was not either of theirs, the Guard's, or the dead man's.

CHAPTER XII

Alvarez telephoned Palma and asked to speak to Superior Chief Salas. A very refined secretary said that Señor Salas was out at a conference. Thank God for small mercies, thought Alvarez. 'Señorita, will you tell Señor Salas that a case which appeared to be suicide may in fact be a murder and I would like authority for a post mortem?'

'In such a case, you should speak to him personally … '

'If you'd be very kind and get on to the Institute of Forensic Anatomy for me and warn them I'll be sending a customer along?' He rang off before she could object.

He opened his bottom desk drawer and brought out the bottle of brandy. It was empty.

*

'Let's go along to the square and have a drink there?' suggested Meegan.

Helen looked across the sitting-room, blinking slightly because the shaft of sunlight which came in through the opened french windows was blinding. 'I've a better idea. Let's stay here and have two drinks.'

His irritation was immediate. 'What's got you so home-loving, all of a sudden? It's not so long ago when you were hardly ever in the house.'

She studied his face which clearly portrayed his strong-willed, stubborn character and saw lines of worry. 'Jim, we've been to the square God knows how many times in the last few days. And when we're there, you seem to be on edge and wanting to get away. People come along to talk and after a bit you're so rude they wonder why they bothered.'

'I can't stand the Boars … '

'They're not the only ones you've been rude to, not by a long chalk. You seem to be wanting to hear something — what? What is it you're so desperate to know?'

He spoke sharply. 'You're imagining things.'

'I'm quite certain I'm not. Why can't you tell me what's the trouble so I can help?'

'I don't need any help.'

'You need something. You've become unapproachable. All right, we've had our ups and downs; what married couple don't? All right, I was a bloody fool to encourage John and then to go to his place. But life was becoming so grim and earnest … '

'Will it help your conscience if I accept that it was my fault from beginning to end?'

'You're not going to make me lose my temper just so that I'll stop bothering you. The hard fact is, it was both our faults, and the fault of this island which breeds situations quicker than mosquitoes. But that's all over and done with. I want to know what's worrying you sick now, right at this moment.'

'It's the same as it was yesterday, last week, last month. I can't move the book along.'

She sighed. 'Your mother always said that if you were really worried you could never help yourself by telling anyone what the trouble was, you just went on and on burning inside.'

'She got in a panic if I didn't confide everything in her — she was one of those mothers who're always scared of losing contact with their children. Pretty soon, of course, she did because it was like being mentally smothered.' He stood up. 'Are you coming with me?'

She sighed. 'All right. But let's go to the Bar Ebor for a change?'

'No.'

'Why not — you used to prefer it? Is it because the English seldom drink there?'

He looked quickly at her and wished her intuitive intelligence were not so sharp.

'What are you trying to learn, Jim? It's something to do with John, isn't it?'

'I couldn't give a damn less about him, now he's dead.'

She shook her head. 'I wish to God your mother hadn't been quite so right,' she said as she stood up.

*

The island became very tristful when there was no sunshine. At dawn on Wednesday, the sky was completely overcast. Colours were muted, houses looked awkward and almost shabby, the mountains were gloomily threatening, and even the bay was cold. Then the sun rose and the daily sea breeze began to shred the clouds which were soon driven across the interior of the island and out to sea to the north. When the harsh sunshine returned colours were once more flamboyant, houses were picturesque, the mountains were welcomingly attractive, and the bay was beautiful.

Alvarez, sweating heavily and short of breath, an ache in his right side gloomily reminding him of an article he had read about arthritic hips, slowly climbed the front stairs in the Guardia post. He went along to his room and slumped down in his chair. After a while he looked at the calendar on the wall and saw, with brief pleasure, that soon it would be the day of the Moors and Christians — a fiesta. Only emergencies prevented his taking the day off on a fiesta.

The telephone rang.

'This is Professor Romero's office,' said a plummy-voiced woman. 'Am I speaking to Inspector Alvarez?'

'Yes, señora.'

'Señorita, please ... The Professor has asked me to speak to you as unfortunately he has not the time himself. The preliminary report on the post mortem carried out on Señor Calvin shows that he died about twenty days previously, but this estimate is not to be taken as exact. The cause of death was asphyxia ... '

'What's that?'

'It is quite certain. He died from asphyxia. All the classic signs were present — cyanosis, petechial haemorrhages, vomit. On top of that, he'd suffered a fracture of the cornu — roughly speaking, the voice-box — and there were bruises caused by fingertips immediately beneath the skin of the neck. He was throttled by manual pressure to his neck.'

Alvarez silently swore.

'As you will know, Inspector, when a man is manually throttled and unless he is incapacitated for any particular reason — the deceased had had no alcohol prior to death — he fights back as violently as he can and usually claws at the other person's hands to try to drag them away from his throat. When he does this, his nails frequently scrape up skin. Under one of the nails of the deceased, the Professor found a very small piece of human flesh — too small for any worthwhile tests to be made on it. Because of the siting of this piece of flesh and because all the other nails were exceptionally clean, the Professor is reasonably certain that the murderer cleaned out the deceased's nails — obviously knowing that any skin under them would point to murder.

'Finally, the extensive wound caused by the shot was inflicted after death.'

'That's quite certain?'

'Quite certain, Inspector ... Not what you expected, I suppose?'

'You can say that again and again.'

'I hope it hasn't given you too much of a headache. Ring back if there are any points you wish to discuss. I can always put them to the Professor when he has a moment to spare.'

'Thanks a lot.'

'I'll see the full written report is in the post inside the next three days ... Goodbye.' She cut the connection.

Sweet Jesus! he thought with gloomy resentment. You wondered why a gun didn't eject a fired cartridge and ended up with a man who'd been killed by throttling, not shooting.

*

Alvarez drove down to the Port, stopping when he reached the supermarket. There was a kiosk outside and he bought himself a double cornet, with one scoop of vanilla ice-cream and one of chocolate. For him, ice-cream was one of the luxuries of the world because when he'd been young there'd been little of it for sale and in any case he couldn't begin to afford it.

He left his car parked where it was and walked past the corner garage and down Calle Bunyola to Collom's house. He stepped through the bead curtain into the entrance room and called out. An elderly woman, dressed in black, came from the back room.

'Good morning,' he said, 'I'm Inspector Alvarez from the Cuerpo de Policia.'

She nodded nervously, then turned and hurried up the stairs.

He stared at the framed painting above the colour television set and thought how nice it was to be able to recognize what he was looking at: there was no need for a visual dictionary with this painting of olive trees and sheep.

From above came the tread of heavy feet, then he heard Collom come down the stairs. Collom was bleary-eyed and his hair had been only roughly combed: a couple of drops of water on his right cheek, just above his beard, showed that he had freshened his face. 'What the hell is it now? I've been out all night looking for fish which seem to have bloody vanished, get back and put my head down, and then you turn up just when I'm dreaming I'm hauling in so many fish the boat near sinks.'

'Maybe you're lucky I interrupted you before it foundered.'

'Sarky bastard, aren't you! Now you're here, I suppose you're thirsty?'

'Of course.'

Collom laughed. 'You're a man after my own heart, know that? I've an idea. You throw up your job — leave it to the people from the Peninsula, they've no pride — and join me fishing.'

'When there aren't enough fish to catch?'

Collom tapped the side of his nose with a thick forefinger. 'Two of us in a bigger boat would find new fish to catch.'

'I reckon I'm too old. In any case, I get sea-sick even when it's calm.'

Collom shrugged his shoulders. 'Don't say you were never offered a respectable job … But now you want a large cognac? And after that, you'll want another?'

'You're reading my thoughts.'

'Let's move into the other room. The bottles are in there and it's less distance to keep walking backwards and forwards.'

The room, shaped like a rectangle which had been pushed over several degrees, was lightly furnished, but what furniture there was was of high quality. Collom noticed Alvarez looking at the settee. 'I had a wonderful catch one day, so I bought that suite for the old lady. She's getting on and needs some comfort.'

'Very filial. It's a great pity that fish have become so much scarcer you can't go on helping her as you'd like.'

Collom laughed again, louder than before. He went over to a small table on which stood several bottles and four glasses, poured out two very large brandies, and handed one glass to Alvarez. 'Sit down, drink up, and tell me what's got you all excited.'

Alvarez sat and drank. Only when his glass was three parts empty did he say: 'I suppose you know that the Englishman, Calvin, was found dead on Sunday?'

'Yeah. Someone said something about it.'

'But you weren't interested enough to listen properly?'

'That's right.'

'It's lucky you're a better fisherman than liar.'

Collom's expression altered and he glared at Alvarez.

'How did you see his death? As bad luck because that was the end of your banker, or good luck because you were scared I was asking too many questions and he might have named you?'

'I didn't give a tinker's piss.'

'Let's have a look at your hands.'

'What the hell for?'

Alvarez stood up and crossed to the chair in which Collom sat. 'Come on, don't be shy.'

Collom very slowly put his glass down on a small table, then even more slowly held out his hands, palms upwards: they were callused, bore numerous small cuts and scars, and were a mahogany colour.

'Turn 'em over.'

On the backs of his hands were more cuts and scars, including a four-centimetre long graze which was partially healed. Alvarez tapped the graze with his forefinger. 'How d'you do that?'

Collom shrugged his shoulders again. 'How in hell would I know? In a boat one's always chopping the hands. What's so bloody special about it?'

Alvarez returned to his chair, picked up his glass, and drank. 'Let's hear where you were on the twenty-first of last month.'

'How in God's name would I know that? D'you think I keep a social diary? I was out fishing, or boozing, or making the widow in the next street.'

'It was a Wednesday.'

'It was a Wednesday! D'you think now I can remember exactly where I was because each Wednesday I go and fish one particular bit of sea? Or I don't go out at all? Listen — the fish don't care what day of the week it is.'

'It wasn't very long after I'd talked to you about smuggling.'

'So?'

'So it'll pay you to remember. Like as not, the Englishman was murdered that day.'

'Murdered?' Collom spoke with loud surprise. 'What are you on about now? He blew his head off with a gun and good riddance.'

'He was throttled. Someone grabbed him by the neck and squeezed and then took his body up into the mountains and used the gun to make like he'd shot himself. Whoever throttled him got clawed before he'd finished the job.'

'And you reckon ... ' Collom stared down at his hands. 'You bloody reckon it was me?'

'I reckon you'll soon be able to remember what you were doing on that Wednesday.'

'If I wanted to do a bloke in, I'd take him out to sea and sink him with an iron bar round his neck and that'd be the end of it. No one wouldn't ever find him.'

'Sure. You're the kind of bloke who does a thing in the quickest and most straightforward way.'

'Well?'

'Only you're no fool. So perhaps you killed him like he was killed to make it seem it couldn't be you … Anyway, it's not all that easy to take a body out to sea and dump it. You've got to get it to the harbour, carry it to the boat, and sail out. Tell me when there's a single moment at the harbour when there's not someone looking all ways and seeing what goes on?'

Collom stood up. 'Give us your glass.'

As Alvarez handed his glass over, he said: 'Have you remembered where you were?'

'Fishing, boozing, or making the widow in the next street.' Collom took the two glasses over to the table and refilled them.

'How much did you owe Calvin when he died?'

'Why should I have owed him a peseta?'

'He'll have paid for the load before you picked it up because the people delivering will have demanded cash. You won't have been able to pay him back until you'd sold the load. If he died in the middle of the operation, you'll be quite rich.'

Collom handed Alvarez a glass and returned to his chair. 'I've never worked with him.'

Alvarez looked wearily bored by the answer, but did not challenge it. He drank, then held the balloon glass in the palm of his hand. 'I need your prints before I go.'

Collom's mother came into the room, her movements nervous and uncertain as if she were worried she were going to be roughly ordered out. She looked at her son, so much larger than she that it was difficult to believe she had once borne him, then at Alvarez. 'I wondered, señor, if you would like a biscuit? I have made some this morning and they're all crispy.'

'There's nothing I'd like more.'

She sighed with relief and hurried away.

Collom spoke with angry disgust. 'Boozing 'em ain't enough now: you've got to feed the bastards as well.'

*

Brenda was lying face upwards on a lilo, twenty metres out from the shore, as she soaked up even more sun.

It was no good shouting, thought Alvarez, because she'd never hear him: close inshore the sea was boiling with children, all of whom were shouting at the tops of their voices. So did he roll up his trousers and take off shoes and socks and wade out? He was all too conscious of the fact that his legs were white and his knees were knobbly and that no man was ever at his best in rolled-up trousers.

A Mallorquin boy of about eight was building a sandcastle immediately to his right. He spoke to the boy. 'How'd you like to make yourself a peseta?'

The boy finished scooping a tunnel before he looked up and said: 'Doing what?'

'Going out to that lady on the lilo, there, and asking her to come ashore because I'd like to have a chat with her.'

The boy grinned with cheeky insolence. 'I'll do it for five pesetas.'

'Five? When I was your age … '

'They hadn't invented money.'

Alvarez took a five-peseta piece from his pocket and handed it over. He'd known the time when one peseta was a third of a man's wages for the day … He smiled. What the hell!

The boy ran into the water, splashing an elderly, pinkskinned man who spoke roughly in German, and flung himself down into the sea to swim the last few metres when the water was just deep enough. He spoke to Brenda, who failed to understand him, then pointed at Alvarez. Brenda paddled the lilo round to face the shore. As soon as she recognized Alvarez, she waved.

He watched her paddle ashore. She looked like that picture of Venus, rising out of the water with a huge shell behind her. By God! she stripped years off a man …

She stepped off the lilo and dragged it ashore. 'Fancy seeing you here! Go and change and come and have a swim.'

'I wish I could, señora … '

'The water's like velvet. And if you haven't a costume handy, I'll lend you one of Steve's. The middle will be a bit tight, that's the only trouble.'

'I think, señora, the middle would be under too much strain for either comfort or safety. I would like to talk to you in the flat, if I may?'

'Sure. I was going to come ashore, anyway.'

He carried the lilo across the road and as he followed her up the stairs he could not stop watching the way her hips moved: seldom had he seen such voluptuous movement. She said they'd sit out and drink on the balcony and went inside, he put the lilo down and sat on one of the canvas chairs and sadly wondered if women ever truly found men voluptuous.

She returned with a tray on which were two glasses, a bottle of brandy, and an insulated ice bowl. 'I guessed you'd have a brandy? With lots of ice? I'm sure it's all right so long as you use lots of ice because then brandy won't do you any harm. That's what John always said, anyway.'

He drank and the brandy was already cold enough to bring out sweat on his face and neck. 'Señora, is Señor Adamson here?'

'No.' She leaned back and faced the sun and her breasts stood very proud and seemingly at risk of escaping from the bikini top. 'To tell the truth, we've been getting on each other's nerves a bit recently so he cleared off for the day.'

'I'm sorry there has been trouble.'

'He can't seem to understand ... ' She became silent for a while, then said: 'I know I'm stupid. John always used to say I was the only person he'd ever met who thought two and two made twenty-two. But even if I am stupid, I don't see why he should get so angry just because I'm upset that he's dead.'

By now, Alvarez was able to follow without too much trouble whom she was talking about.

'After all, he was my husband. And one can't lose a husband without being just a little upset, can one?'

'I should think not, señora.'

'All right, he chased after other women and that made me spitting mad, but I think he just couldn't help it. Some men are like that. They see a fresh body and they're off. God knows why. After all, we're all the same underneath our clothes, aren't we?'

'More or less, señora.'

'Still, he'll have to get over it and if he doesn't, he can take a powder. I just can't stand sulky bad tempers.'

'Does Señor Adamson have a job?'

'Steve?' she laughed. 'Work and him don't adjust. No, he's one of those blokes made for lounging around, looking divinely handsome. He's a real knock-out in a dinner-jacket. And can he dance! Talk about sex on the move.'

'Señora, I fear I have something more to tell you about your husband.'

She shifted in the chair and stared at him, her deep blue eyes suddenly filled with worry. 'Is it something rather nasty? Then have you got to tell me? I do so hate hearing nasty things.'

'He did not commit suicide. Your husband was murdered.'

'Murdered? ... I'm glad.'

'You're glad?'

'John was a fighter and that's what I most liked about him. And I don't mean him and me fighting like cat and dog because that's different. I mean taking the world on and not giving way to anyone. When you told me he'd committed suicide ... it just wasn't him. It turned him into someone who'd given in and it was terrible to think of him as that.'

'The fact he was murdered, señora, means someone murdered him.'

'Well, even I can see that!'

'What I'm indicating is that now I have to find out who killed him. It may make life unpleasant for some people.'

'So it damn well should.' She spoke with sudden fierceness.

'Perhaps you will help me? Do you remember that I showed you the note that was left in the typewriter?'

'Yes.'

'Do you think it could have been forged? That someone else wrote it, then imitated the signature?'

She thought about that. 'Not in a thousand years,' she said decisively.

'I think, señora, that that is probably what happened, however.'

'The way it was written was exactly how he'd have written it — all snarky. I could even hear him saying it in his laughing voice.'

'Yet surely someone wishing to imitate what he might write if he were going to commit suicide would have written just like that?'

'You mean, put two fingers up at the world and deliberately jeer at the conventions? ... They'd have had to know him pretty well to get it so right.'

He nodded.

'But none of his friends would kill him. It's a ridiculous thing to say.'

'Unfortunately, it has to be said ... Señora, could you swear that the signature definitely was not forged?'

'Well, it ... Look, I'm sure it wasn't. But I can't say for absolute certain, can I?'

'Very true. You are being most helpful.'

She said suddenly, surprise roughening her voice: 'I think that you're thinking maybe Steve or I could have done it.'

'Only a man would have had the strength to throttle Señor Calvin.'

'It wasn't Steve. He hasn't the courage to do a thing like that. Don't take any notice of the way he acts or talks. I'm telling you, he hasn't the courage. If he says something really wild, it's meaningless ... '

He interrupted her. 'Señora, I will question him whatever you say.'

'But it couldn't have been Steve. Why would he ever do such a thing?'

'Your husband was in danger of being forced back to England where he would have been arrested for currency manipulations. If he had been fined very heavily, he might have had to sell everything in this country and somehow take the money back to England to pay the fine and so avoid further imprisonment. Then there would have been nothing here to repay you all the money of yours he had had.'

'You think that Steve and I could ever have worked out anything that complicated?' She laughed.

She sounded genuinely amused, he thought. Yet he suspected that long ago she had discovered the value of appearing more naively simple than she was ... And if one stopped to think about it, two and two could be said to make twenty-two.

It was clear that, despite whatever rows they had been having recently, she was still very fond of Adamson. In that case, she would probably be only too glad — since women always put their loves before their loyalties — to divert suspicion away from Adamson, even if to do so was to endanger a friend. 'Señora, I understand all you've said. So now I need to know who else to question. Tell me, did Señor Calvin become very friendly with many women in the past few months? And have you recently met any man who is a husband of such a woman who has been scratched, especially on the back of his hands, or who has had other injuries?'

CHAPTER XIII

There had been a breeze in the Port, but up in the valley there was none and the heat, trapped between the two ranges of mountains, was greater than it had been all that summer. Sheep, goats, and the occasional cow or mule, all huddled under what shade they could find, lacking the energy even to forage. Only the vultures and a solitary golden eagle, spiralling high above the mountains, seemed to be unaffected.

The Seat dropped into a large pot-hole which Alvarez failed to avoid and there was a metallic crunch which made him swear. A little further along the very steep, rough dirt track leading up to the rock shelf on the mountain, one of the front tyres struck a large stone, the steering-wheel jerked and the car was momentarily deflected towards the edge. Sweet Mary, preserve me! he prayed, not daring to look right towards the precipitous slope on that side because heights turned him into a coward. He should have walked up the path he and the shepherd had used before, but the thought of such a climb in the heat had been too much.

The zig-zagging track came to an end. He climbed out of the car and wondered how he was ever going to get it back down. Perhaps he would abandon it.

Climbing, he skirted a large, straggly spurge bush only to scratch his right ankle on a spiny creeper. Jumping aside, he stepped on some loose stones and felt them rattle away so that his mind was filled with visions of a rock avalanche. In a state of near panic, he reached the rock shelf.

He took a handkerchief from his pocket and mopped his face and neck and tried to regain his breath. Then he began to search the shelf systematically and exhaustively. He found marks, probably recent, possibly made by shoes, but these were meaningless and it was impossible to know whether they had been made before the body was found. There was a scrap of plastic, wedged behind a small piece of rock which was up against the rock face, but this again was of no significance. The rock face still bore the signs of the shooting, otherwise it was clear.

He leaned against the rock and lit a cigarette. He had been pretty certain he could not have missed anything of consequence the previous time, but had had to check. He stared out across the valley and once again the scene filled him with a wonderful sense of peace and the fact that he stood within a couple of metres of where there had been a murdered body produced no sense of discord.

When his cigarette was finished, he walked over to the edge of the shelf, dropped the butt and stamped it out, then kicked it over the edge. Had Calvin been strangled up here and then the scene set for the bogus suicide? Had he been strangled elsewhere and then his body brought up? If the former, what had he and his murderer been doing up here? If the latter, why: why not have left the body very much nearer Ca'n Adeane? He'd originally presumed that the suicide had taken place on the shelf because Calvin had wanted a last look at beauty before he blasted himself into the unknown. Since that was nonsense, why had the body been brought so far unless for the obvious reason of hiding it for as long as possible? Then why leave the fake suicide note where it would be found immediately?

After a time he returned to the car. He studied the maximum width available to him for turning, looked with horror at the slope on the outside of the path, wondered about backing down the slope and knew that anything was preferable to that.

It took him nine locks to turn the car and when the last one was over he was sweating so heavily that he actually felt momentarily cold as the sweat evaporated. He lit another cigarette, promised himself a really large brandy at the first available opportunity, and began the drive down.

The shepherd, with his dog and his flock of sheep, was just along the track from his house. 'Been back up there again, eh? Didn't walk this time, but you ought to have done. Nothing like a good walk to take the fat off your belly.'

'How d'you know where I've been?' asked Alvarez curiously.

'Got eyes, ain't I? I looks and I sees. I don't keep me animals healthy without looking all the time.' He waved his stick at a sheep, which moved back towards the main body of the flock while the dog came to a standing position and waited for the order which did not follow.

'You've just seen me in the car going along the dirt track to the rock shelf?'

''Course I did.'

'If you've got eyes that good, you must know a lot of what goes on about here?'

'I knows as much as the next man. And a little bit more.'

'Then maybe you've seen another car drive up that path not so very long ago?'

'Maybe I have.' The shepherd hawked and spat.

Alvarez waited, showing not the slightest hint of impatience.

'I see a car like yours.'

'A Seat six hundred?'

'How do I know what kind it is? I ain't interested in what a car is unless it runs over one of me sheep.'

'When you charge the driver three times what the beast is worth?'

The shepherd cackled with laughter. 'They've got more money than sense, ain't they, so where's the harm?'

'No harm. What colour was this car?'

The shepherd thought for some time. 'It were light.'

'White, grey, fawn?'

'It were light-coloured. I don't know no more than that.'

'How long ago do you reckon you saw it?'

'I isn't never worried about time. When it's light I gets up, when it's dark I goes to bed.'

'But you'll have some idea of how many days or weeks ago you saw it?'

'It weren't all that long ago. Like as not, a week or two.'

'Do you often see cars going up that track?'

'Ain't seen another since I don't know when.'

'Did you get a sight of who was in it?'

'With me that far away? You must think I've eyes like a hawk's.'

'Why not? You're an old buzzard.'

The simple joke so amused the shepherd that he laughed himself into a coughing fit and Alvarez had to thump him on the back.

'Why d'you keep asking questions?' asked the shepherd, when he was once more able to speak.

'Because the Englishman was murdered and didn't commit suicide. Someone throttled him.'

The shepherd stared at Alvarez. 'Him with half his head blown off and you talk about being throttled? How bloody daft can you get?' He was very annoyed and he turned his back on Alvarez, whistled the dog into action, and began to move the flock on.

*

Alvarez compared Collom's fingerprints with the unidentified print taken from the shotgun and found that none matched. He sighed, rested his arms on the desk, his head on his arms, and went to sleep.

The telephone woke him, as it had so often done recently. Resentfully, he answered it.

'I'm speaking from the Department of Graphology. I've compared the crime signature with the specimen signatures and although it's impossible to be definite on the strength of just one crime signature, I'd say it's genuine.'

'Did you say genuine?'

'You sound surprised?'

'If it is genuine, I can't make head or tail of things.'

'Sorry to confuse the issue … There you are, then. No certainty, but great probability.'

'Thanks,' said Alvarez, wondering what he was thanking the other for.

After replacing the receiver, he stared at the top of his desk. How could the signature be genuine? One of the suspects had surely to be either a first-class forger or else to have access to the work of one. Adamson?

He went back to sleep.

*

From the next room came the sounds of Antonia's making the bed. It was wasted effort, thought Meegan. Like all Mallorquins, she never tucked the bedclothes in and so invariably Helen remade the bed. Wasted effort was something about which he was a bit of an expert. He looked away from the typewriter and round at the shelf on which were all his published books. There were nine hardback titles and one paperback translation from Holland. (The Dutch were still very sympathetic towards the English.)

He could still remember the sense of exaltation he had felt when he'd heard his first book had been accepted. Success and fortune: move over Graham Greene, one step down the ladder of fame, Angus Wilson. He could also still remember his great worry: would the critics appreciate the fact that the novel was at two levels — for those with the intelligence to see below the surface? Should he not at least have hinted at this in the blurb, despite the publisher's Philistine comment on pretentiousness? … He could have saved himself an awful lot of worry. The only critic who reviewed the book in print worked for a paper published in a town in Yorkshire that had taken him ages to find on a map — and quite clearly that critic hadn't even scratched the surface of the first level.

His ability, of very dubious merit, of being able to stand aside from himself and study his life with mocking criticism let him laugh (at the same time as he damn near cried) over the way in which he always set out to write a work that would illuminate some of the basic truths of human nature, but ended up by asking 'Who's for tennis?' If he had had the private income that Helen had, so that he was not writing for money, could he have written something worthwhile? He still liked to believe so. Perhaps because he knew there was no chance of his ever having a private income since his only wealthy relative had died eight years before and left her fortune to charity, despite all the loving attention of her nephews and nieces.

He lit a cigarette. Maybe he should wear a clown's hat when he worked? Yet wasn't there just a little merit in having an ambition, even if life had proved over and over again that such ambition was a banana skin?

He heard a car come to a squeaking halt and identified it as their Seat. A minute later, Helen came into the room, a plastic carrier-bag in her hand. 'I've a terrible confession to make and will you forgive me?'

He leaned back in his chair. 'Are you asking for absolution in advance?'

'I want you to promise faithfully not to be annoyed, not to be nasty to me, and not to go into one of your moods when you hear what I've done.'

'You're getting me really worried. Have you knocked a Guardia down with the car? Do we need to flee the island immediately?'

'I've bought two hundred grammes of smoked salmon from the supermarket for supper because I decided we'd got to celebrate.'

'Celebrate what?'

'I haven't the slightest idea, which means we've got to work extra hard at celebrating. And to help, I bought a bottle of champagne. And just so life doesn't fall flat afterwards, a couple of steaks.'

'Sheer hedonistic profligacy!'

'And why not?' She kissed him lightly. 'It does one good to pander to one's excesses now and then ... I'll go and put the champagne in the fridge to cool.'

The world, he thought, loved an irony. When they'd nothing serious to worry about, they'd made certain they didn't enjoy life by rowing: now, at a time of sharp, dangerous tension, they were finding fun and a great deal to enjoy.

They both heard a car draw up outside. 'I wonder who's calling in working hours?' she said. 'I thought we'd got everyone trained not to do that.'

'It's no longer working hours. My boss has just given me the rest of the day off.'

She kissed him again. 'I'm beginning to like your boss ... I'll go and see who it is and chase them off because I feel like having my husband to myself.'

After she'd gone, he pulled the sheet of paper out of the typewriter and placed it on top of the others from the same chapter. There were a hundred and twenty-five pages to go now. Had he enough plot left? ... To hell with it: today was for celebrating, leave the morrow for worrying.

He waited, hoping Helen was getting rid of the visitor or visitors, but when she didn't return he went along the passage, past the kitchen in which Antonia was now enthusiastically, if somewhat inexpertly, washing up and into the sitting-room. He was shocked to see that Helen was looking frightened, although there was nothing apparently frightening about the squat, heavily built, stolid-looking man who immediately made him think of Millet.

Helen said quickly: 'Jim, this is Inspector Alvarez from the local CID. He's come because of John. He says John didn't commit suicide, he was murdered.'

'He what?'

'He was throttled, señor,' said Alvarez. 'But only at the post mortem did we discover this thing.'

'But we heard the gun was in his hands and he'd left a letter?'

'Attempts to make his death look like a suicide. By luck, however, the truth has been discovered.'

'Luck for whom?'

'An interesting question, señor. Certainly not for the murderer.'

'And have you discovered who that is?'

'Not yet, and I fear it is going to take a little time. There will have to be many enquiries.'

'Have a drink?' suggested Helen suddenly, almost breathlessly.

'Please don't derange yourself ... '

She tried to speak lightly. 'I'm dying for a drink. Say yes and then Jim can't refuse me one.'

'In that case, señora, I would very much like a brandy. But only a small one.'

'Good. And please sit down ... Jim, I'll have a sweet vermouth.'

She needed to relax, thought Meegan as he crossed to the bottle chest. For the moment, she was working too hard at being the perfect hostess. He poured out drinks and added ice, passed the glasses round. He sat down in the armchair opposite Alvarez and raised his glass: 'Your health.'

'And yours, señor. To admit the truth, this is not my first today, but it is surely going to be the most welcome.'

Curiosity, Meegan decided, was in order. 'You said you'd come here because of John and that he'd been murdered?'

'You will now understand that I have to find out who murdered him.'

'Of course. But what I don't get is why you've come here?'

'If I may put it this way. First, I must discover who obviously did not commit the murder, then maybe I will be able to say who did.'

'All right. Now you can eliminate two people: neither of us killed him.' Meegan spoke challengingly.

'There is no question of a lady having done it, señor, although I believe a lady may well be able to assist me. That is why I should like to ask the señora a question.'

'If she knows nothing ... '

'Don't be silly, Jim,' cut in Helen. 'Of course I'll help all I can.'

'Thank you, señora. Please excuse my curiosity in matters which are private, but is it true that you were friendly with Señor Calvin?'

Meegan spoke with sharp anger. 'Who the hell says that?'

'I have heard ... '

'From whom?'

'Señor, I hear many things and often it is better not to say who told me.'

'I knew John,' said Helen. She was sitting very upright in her chair.

'Was he a friend?'

'Not in the way you're suggesting.'

'I hope I am suggesting nothing. Please tell me, have you ever visited his house on your own?'

She gripped her glass so tightly that her knuckles whitened. 'No.'

'If someone says you had lunch with him not very long before he died, that person is either mistaken or lying?' There was a silence, broken when Antonia came out of the kitchen, wished them all good afternoon, and left, seemingly unaware of the tension in the sitting-room.

Alvarez spoke quietly. 'Please, señora, understand that I do not wish to know anything unnecessary, but for now I cannot say what is necessary and what is not. If you will tell me the truth, I will be able to sort things out and afterwards forget all that is unnecessary. But if I am not told and I have to find out these things, perhaps other people learn them as well and do not forget so quickly.'

She ran her tongue along her lips and looked at her husband. 'I … All right, I did have lunch with him. But it was only the once and there was nothing else to it.'

'She didn't have an affair with him,' said Meegan harshly. 'It was just a lunch.'

'With his … ' Alvarez hesitated, as if wondering how best to put the question. 'With his reputation, señor, perhaps you were not very pleased by the meeting?'

'Why the hell should I have worried since I trusted her completely? And what's this got to do with his death?'

'I have to understand the background to his murder and if there are people who might have liked him dead, I have to talk to them to discover how much they would have liked this.'

'Since I trusted my wife, I'd no reason for wishing him anything.'

'Believe me, señor, that makes me happy. Now, I have only to ask one or two questions more, take your fingerprints, and everything is over.'

'My … my fingerprints? Why?'

'I need them.'

'Like hell. I'm not giving them as if I were some bloody crook.'

'Señor, I can understand your attitude, I believe. The English do not suffer things like identity cards and the police may not worry them unless they get permission. But here, in Spain, we arrange matters in a slightly different style and therefore you will be very wise to give me your prints when I ask for them. And please do not forget that if you have a Residencia you will already have given them voluntarily.'

'You still haven't explained why you want them?'

'I have a print I wish to identify. When I discover that it is not yours, I can look elsewhere.'

'Where's it from?'

'It was on the gun which was supposed to have killed the señor.'

'My print couldn't possibly be on that.'

'Then you will surely be pleased to prove how right you are? I have the equipment in the car and later we will take them.'

He seemed so pleasant and benign that it came as a shock to discover a trace of smooth steel underneath.

'Señor, will you now tell me where you were on the twenty-first of July?'

'How would I know that now?' replied Meegan, at the same time as Helen said, 'He was with me.'

Alvarez appeared not to have noticed their different answers. 'The twenty-first was a Wednesday — exactly three weeks ago, as a matter of fact. I know it is very difficult to remember what happened three weeks ago, but perhaps you will be able to do so?'

'We spent the whole day together,' said Helen.

'You are very certain, señora. Perhaps you have a reason for that?'

'As a matter of fact, I have. We'd had a pretty bitter row, but made it up Tuesday night and we spent all Wednesday together, finding out how stupid we'd been.'

'Thank you, that is very clear.' Alvarez spoke to Meegan again. 'Señor, I am a simple man, who unfortunately often asks questions very bluntly because I can think of no other way of putting them, even though I perhaps upset people with my bluntness. So having excused myself, please now tell me if about three weeks ago you were suffering from any slight physical injury?'

'None at all.'

'You had no scratches on your hands? No bruising on your face?'

'I've just said not.'

'He's had nothing like that,' said Helen. 'D'you understand, nothing at all.'

'Señora, I think you understand why I ask. But do you also understand that you must answer exactly? Because if I learn that your husband did have some slight injury, I will begin to wonder why both he and you deny it and you will realize what answer I will give myself.'

'He has not had any kind of an injury.'

Alvarez nodded, but it was not a gesture suggesting he accepted her answer, merely one acknowledging the fact that she would not alter it. He spoke once more to Meegan. 'Señor, I am told you write books. Of what kind are they?'

'Very ordinary, according to most people and one critic.'

'Do they deal with crime and criminals?'

'Sometimes.'

'So you understand a little of the subject. And, perhaps, you have books which tell you how a policeman does his job?'

'Yes.'

'It is good to hear that you get your facts correct.' He scratched his forehead. 'I am trying to discover some facts about Señor Calvin's gun, which looks to me to be a very nice one. I believe there are very big shoots in England, with lots of pheasants ...'

'I don't know anything about guns or shooting.'

'Not even how to load ... '

'Nothing. And I didn't use the gun to try to fake the suicide.'

'Then now I have asked all my questions and I can leave the house — Señora, I apologize sincerely for disturbing you as I have. Señor, if you will come out with me to the car I will quickly take your fingerprints.' He stood up and left his glass, with just the polite amount of brandy remaining, on the nearest small table.

'Jim isn't ...' began Helen in a high-pitched voice, then stopped. She stared helplessly at Alvarez.

'Believe me, I will do all I can to cause as little trouble as is possible.'

Outside, the heat gripped the two men and they were both sweating by the time they reached Alvarez's Seat, parked in the shade. From all around came the shrill cries of cicadas, and a very large grasshopper, disturbed by them, whirred through the air.

'It is as hot as I can ever remember it,' said Alvarez. 'Work is not much fun in such heat.' He smiled, his heavy face relaxing. 'But perhaps if I tell the whole truth, work is never fun, hot or cold ... I will get the things out of the car, but first there is a question I wished to ask but which I forgot. What kind of car do you have?'

'A Seat six hundred.'

'The same as mine. I hope it is in better condition?'

'Worse.'

'That is difficult to believe.'

'What's it matter what state it's in?'

'Surely it must be quite immaterial,' replied Alvarez blandly, 'but when I was training I was taught that no detective could ever discover too many facts, no matter how irrelevant they seemed. I've never been able to forget that advice, although I forget many things, and now I fill my head with useless facts. What colour is this car?'

'I've a right to know why … '

'Señor, in this country foreigners often do not have as many rights as they have at home, but we try always to be courteous and not to make unnecessary trouble. Now, if you will tell me the colour?'

'White.'

'Thank you.' Alvarez turned, opened the passenger door of his Seat and brought out a very battered plastic case which he put on the roof. From this he took an ink pad, two carbon forms, and some cleansing tissues: the air was so still that the tissues lay motionless. 'Perhaps you remember how one takes your prints? I hold your finger and roll it from side to side on the ink pad and then transfer it to the form and roll it again … Please be relaxed, because then we do not smudge anything.'

As Meegan's prints were taken, he wondered if the detective noticed how much his hands were sweating and whether he would realize that this was not solely because of the heat.

'That is fine, señor. Not a single smudge. Now if you will use the tissues you will find you can clean off all the mess.' He handed the tissues across.

Meegan cleaned his fingers. Alvarez repacked the case and put it back on the passenger seat.

'Thank you again, señor, for all your help.' He shook hands. He climbed into the car and started the engine, reversed in a wide arc to the edge of the turning circle, and then drove up the slip road.

Meegan watched the car out of sight, heard it come to a squeaky halt at the T-junction, pull out, and carry on round and down to the road out of the urbanizacion. For the most part, the detective had seemed courteous but totally uninspired, yet more than once his manner had hinted at a different character underneath. Were the hints misleading? Was he sharp and intelligent or merely sharp and prepared when necessary to prove he'd the power to push people around? Had he accepted all the answers he'd been given, or had he mentally filed some of them away for further examination?

He returned into the house, to find that Helen hadn't moved. Her expression was strained, frightened. 'Thank God that's got rid of him … Jim, you must tell me.'

'I reckon I've answered enough questions.'

'How did you get that bruise on your face?'

121

'Exactly as I said. I walked into a branch in the dark.'

She seemed to shiver.

'Forget it, darling. He had to try to make some sort of a showing. I'll bet you anything you like that most of the time he'd no more idea of why he was asking the questions than we had ... Come on, buck up. Remember we were getting ready to celebrate with smoked salmon, champagne, and steaks?'

Her expression didn't alter.

CHAPTER XIV

Alvarez entered the square and looked towards the church to check the time. He saw the ice-cream stall. No more ice-creams — the shepherd was right and he was putting on far too much weight. Weight was bad for the blood pressure. But was ice-cream, in fact, fattening?

He bought only a small cornet and congratulated himself on resisting temptation. He ate it, then crossed the square which was attractively speckled by winking shadows as the light from the overhead lamps played through the slowly moving leaves of the plane trees.

The first person he met in the bar of the Club Llueso was Antonio Vives. 'There you are!' shouted Vives. 'God, it's hot! If they opened the furnace doors of hell it couldn't get any hotter.'

'If that's how you comfort yourself, forget it. When you get down there you'll remember this as the Ice Age.' He slumped down in the chair opposite Vives.

'Two cognacs,' Vives shouted at the barman. 'Large ones.'

'Not for me,' said Alvarez. 'I'll stick with coffee.'

'At this time of night? What are you trying to do to yourself?'

'Slim.'

'Why?'

'Fat's bad for the health.'

'So's everything that's worthwhile. What's eating you? You sound like you need a woman.'

'Ever known him when he didn't?' demanded Rosallio, joining in the conversation. 'His big trouble is, the women don't need him.' He sat down at the table.

'I'm telling you, he's just refused a cognac. He wants coffee only.'

'And you believed him? There's one born every minute.'

'Says cognac's making him too fat.'

Rosallio studied Alvarez. 'Too fat for what?' He roared with laughter.

The waiter came to the table with two glasses of brandy and Rosallio reached out for one. 'If you're not drinking, Enrique, I am. I've a thirst that would empty Miguel's well.' He drank. 'By God! there's nothing like a cognac to put life back into a man.' He dug his elbow into Alvarez's side. 'Pity you don't drink yourself a new life: you look like you need it bad.' He laughed again.

Vives paid the waiter. 'Don't you want another cognac, seeing there's three of you now?' asked the waiter.

Vives jerked his thumb at Alvarez. 'He's not drinking.'

The waiter looked curiously at Alvarez. 'Sorry to hear you're ill, Enrique. Hope it's nothing serious?'

There were times, thought Alvarez sourly, as he reached over and picked up Vives's brandy, when good intentions were as much use as confetti at a funeral.

Rosallio's laughter boomed round the room. 'Giving up drinking! Him! Just because he's getting as fat as a pig? I'll tell you, if he was as fat as two pigs, he'd go on drinking. Think a mangy old leopard like him is going to change its spots?' He spoke to the waiter. 'Bring another round.'

Two and a half hours later, Alvarez walked slowly up Calle Juan Rives and struggled to focus his eyes so that the two street lights merged into one. Mournfully, he cursed himself for having bought that chocolate ice-cream. That was what was responsible.

He tried to open the wooden front doors of his cousin's house and after he'd pulled and pushed for a time he came to the conclusion that they were locked. He searched his pockets and his clumsy fingers found and finally subdued the key and he unlocked the wooden doors. The glass doors inside were unlocked. He went inside, locked the wooden doors, shut the glass doors, and congratulated himself on being a man who could really hold his liquor. He tripped over his feet and crashed to the floor.

The government should forbid the sale of ice-cream. He stood up unsteadily. How could any leopard change its spots when temptation surrounded it? And to tell the truth, that was a bloody silly saying because had any leopard ever actually changed its spots?

He climbed the stairs, grateful for the wooden rail, and went carefully along the short passage to his bedroom. He slumped down on the bed. The ceiling light began to dance around so he closed his eyes. He'd go on the wagon, never even look at a brandy again, never, never suffer the humiliation of not being in full control of his senses ... Something about that leopard worried him, but when he tried to visualize the animal he imagined their neighbour's tom cat. He hated cats.

*

Alvarez drove up the winding road to Ca'n Setonia and parked. The front of the house was a blaze of colour, thanks to a deep red and salmon pink bougainvillaea. Foreigners might have destroyed much of the natural beauty of the island around the coast with their greed for the sun, but they had returned just a little cultivated beauty with their gardens.

The ground sloped sharply and he had to walk downhill for three metres before turning on to the level path of the front door. Hanging from a wrought iron lion's head on the door was a rectangle of cardboard, headed 'Messages', to which were clipped several sheets of paper and a pencil. He longed to write 'Go home' in block capitals. Instead, he rang the bell.

Amanda, wearing a brightly coloured frock that suited her somewhat juvenile, bubbly looks, opened the door. He introduced himself.

Immediately she spoke with nervous speed. 'Do come in. Into the sitting-room. We love the view from there — Perce says ... ' She became uncomfortably silent as she realized she'd completely lost the thread of what she had been about to say. Her nervousness increased and she fidgeted with an edge of her dress.

'Is your husband in, señora?'

'Not at the moment. He's gone down to the Port.'

'Would you prefer me to leave and come back when he is here?'

'Yes ... No. What I really mean is, no.'

'Are you sure that would not be more convenient?'

She said abruptly: 'It's much better if you stay.' She turned and hurried into the sitting-room.

As soon as he entered, she said, in a bright, hostess voice: 'Isn't it a magnificent view?'

'Indeed it is, señora.'

'The mountains are so lovely, especially in the early morning or at sunset. Do you like mountains?'

'Yes, I do.'

'Please sit down. Anywhere you like. The chairs are quite comfortable.'

They both sat.

She left her dress alone and rested her hands in her lap, but seconds later she began to twist a button backwards and forwards. 'When people in England hear we live in Mallorca, they turn up their noses and talk about concrete jungles. I tell them, they don't know what they're talking about. This end of the island is just beautiful. All the mountains, the fields, the drystone walls, the old farmhouses … But you know all about that, don't you? I mean, you live here.'

'Yes, señora,' he answered politely.

'I was just being stupid.' She looked at him, drew a deep breath, then said abruptly: 'Why are you here?'

'I am enquiring into the death of Señor Calvin.'

'Is it true he was murdered and didn't commit suicide?'

'Quite true.'

'And you've come here … because you've heard … What have you heard?'

'That you were a friend of Señor Calvin,' he answered quietly. To his surprise, from the moment he said that she became very much more composed.

'Who told you that?'

'Señora, I have made so many enquiries that I cannot remember exactly.'

'And you think my knowing John is important?'

'It could be.'

'Then you've got to understand it's not quite like some people think.'

'It isn't?'

'Look — if I tell you the absolute truth, do you have to tell anyone else?'

'If it proves to be of no importance, certainly not.'

'Not even Perce?'

'Señora, it will be a secret between us.'

'Then I'm going to tell you. I've never been really friendly with John. He kind of amused me, because he could be such fun and he was a really terrible flatterer — knew just how to say what one wanted to hear, if you know what I mean? But I never … I didn't have an affair with him. I only tried to make Perce think I had so I could deny it. Can you understand?'

'Not really, señora.'

'It's rather embarrassing to explain.' Her blue eyes were deeply troubled as she stared at him. 'You see, I met someone and … and we fell in love: terribly in love. I did everything I could to hide it, but Perce began to be suspicious and tried to catch me out. I'm so hopeless a liar that I knew if ever he guessed at the name of the man he'd challenge me and I wouldn't be able to hide the truth, so I deliberately let John get friendly at parties because then Perce would be sure it was him. That's what Perce did think, but when he accused me of having an affair with John I just laughed at him and he pretty well stopped being suspicious because I'm so terrible a liar he had to believe me and so he decided he'd been making a fool of himself with all his suspicions. So you see, I really can't help you over John. And now there's no need at all for you to speak to Perce.'

'I am sorry, señora, but I fear I must still speak to him.'

'Why? I've explained everything … '

'But suppose he didn't disbelieve his own suspicions quite as thoroughly as you think he did?'

She began to fiddle once more with a button on her dress. 'Suppose he didn't? You can't really think that even if he'd been absolutely convinced it was John, he'd have gone out and murdered him from jealousy?'

'I don't know. But I have to check all possibilities.'

'Perce kill someone? He's only enough courage for shouting at women,' she said, with sudden and withering contempt.

'Nevertheless, I must question him.'

'Then you … you're saying you will tell him what I've just told you?'

'No, señora, I am saying nothing of the sort. You have my promise that your husband will learn nothing from me unless it becomes absolutely essential.'

'I … I don't want to hurt Perce — even if he likes hurting me. He'd never get over the humiliation.'

How in the name of hell did one ever learn to understand the English with their sentimental hypocrisy? he wondered irritatedly.

'And I can't let Perce hurt my … my friend. He's married with a wife who's a cripple and he has to spend all his money in supporting her. He'll never leave her because that would be so unfair to her — otherwise we'd have gone off together.'

Cheerfully humiliating Perce! The worst part of their hypocrisy was the way in which they claimed merit from their twisted actions. 'When will the señor be back?'

'He said he'd return at twelve.'

'Then I shall call back to see him. One last thing, señora. Have you any idea where you and your husband were on the twenty-first of July, a Wednesday?'

She stood up and crossed to the large desk. 'Perce keeps a diary of absolutely everything he does. Ask him what he was doing eight years ago and he'll give you chapter and verse.' She opened a large desk diary and checked through the pages. 'We can't have been doing anything much because all he's written down are the temperature, weather, and that he drove down to the Port and collected the papers in the morning.'

'You weren't with him?'

She shook her head. 'I can't have been or he would have put that down.'

'Might you have been with your friend for some part of the day?'

'I might have been. I can't tell you.'

'One last question, señora. How many cars have you and what are they?'

'We've got a Renault and a Citroën. The Citroën's mine.'

He thanked her, promised once more he would say nothing to her husband unless absolutely forced to do so, and then left. Thank God he'd never married, he thought, as he drove slowly down the road with its three acute hairpin bends. Then he chided himself. If he had married, he would have married Juana-Maria and not in a thousand, thousand years would she have betrayed him, not even with a glance, let alone her body. Only the English treated marriage as a bad joke because they were hypocritical heathens.

He reached the Llueso/Puerto Llueso road and turned left to the Port. He parked in Calle Bunyola, immediately outside Collom's house.

Collom's mother said: 'Señor, my son is out in his boat and, with God's help, catching many fish. I cannot tell when he will be back.'

She was dressed all in black because she was a widow and he saw in her all the tremendous moral strength and fierce loyalty of the Mallorquin peasant. She would never have visited other beds when her husband was out in his boat. All her life, she had known a sharp, unambiguous line between right and wrong and had never ever dreamed of crossing that line. He smiled warmly at her. 'That's all right. I'll have a word with him some other time.'

She hesitated, but the sudden friendly warmth of his smile freed her tongue. 'Señor, I must tell you. Pedro is a really good boy. Ever since his father died, he has looked after me and given me a wonderful home and if ever he marries — which God willing he will do — he has promised I shall live with him and his wife. He cannot do a great wrong to anyone.'

Alvarez nodded.

'You do not understand,' she said, peering intently at his face. 'You think me an old woman who's too fond of her only son. I love Pedro, I am mightily proud of Pedro. But I have eyes and a mind and I know him as he is. He can be wild — Sweet Holy Mother, how wild! — but he cannot be wicked. Perhaps he has sold a few cigarettes … ' Her voice died away. Then she spoke fiercely. 'What fisherman from this port has never caught anything but fish? Tell me that.'

'Few.'

'But to kill a man when it is not in the heat of an argument, to strangle him as if he were an unwanted puppy … Señor , that is not Pedro. Now, do you understand?'

'Perfectly.'

'Then remember what I have just said.'

'I will remember it exactly. Now tell me something: has Pedro a car?'

'Indeed. He bought it to take me to see my brother, the one who lives near Laraix and suffers the devil's torments from arthritis. Nine years younger than me, but I'll outlast him to the grave … I want to see Pedro marry soon and stop being so wild. There is a widow not very far away … Whore! Jezebel! He needs a nice girl. Then I will be able to lie down and let the Good Lord take me to meet Rafael. He died fifteen years ago: that is a long time.'

'A very long, sad time, señora.' Alvarez was respectfully silent for a time. 'Señora, this car that Pedro has bought you — I suppose it is a nice small one, cheap on petrol?'

'Cheap? May the saints preserve me, but my son is a fool when it comes to money. Money, he says, is made for spending. Save it, I beg him: next year may be the year of the lean cows. But he just spends and spends … Colour television set, this enormous French car when there are only the two of us to sit in it when we visit my poor brother, and who knows how much goes to that painted harlot? Spend less and keep money under the mattress, I tell him. But he just laughs.'

'It's the way all the youngsters look at things today.'

'It'll do them no good.' She sighed. 'But you can't tell them. They have to learn and be hurt.'

He agreed, they had to learn and be hurt. He said he must go and she refused to let him leave until she'd given him a long, rolled-over pastry filled with the jam known as angel's hair, and this gift suddenly and poignantly reminded him of his mother, who had never known security or comfort, but who had cooked better than anyone else in the world, even Juana-Maria.

He drove down to the harbour and parked in front of the harbourmaster's office on the eastern arm. The office consisted of two rooms, an inner and an outer one, and in the outer room a man with very long hair and an overflowing moustache was working.

'You want to know whether the motor-cruiser *Felicity* cleared harbour on the twenty-first of last month? Hang on a sec and I'll find out.' He yawned.

Alvarez yawned. He turned and stared out of the window and watched a yacht move astern from the quay and turn to make for the harbour entrance. Could anything be more peaceful than to set sail in one's own yacht, leaving all one's problems ashore?

'The *Felicity* left harbour on the twenty-first at twelve-zero-five hours and returned on the twenty-second at eleven-seventeen hours.'

'Thanks a lot.' Alvarez scratched his right ear. 'No idea who was on her, I suppose?'

'Couldn't tell you that, no.'

'Or where she was bound?'

'She reported her destination as Menorca.'

Alvarez thanked the other and went outside into the burning sunshine.

CHAPTER XV

'Listen,' said Adamson fiercely, 'I didn't knock the old bastard off.'

Alvarez stared across the sitting-room of the flat, in its usual state of untidiness. Adamson, he thought, was showing signs of strain.

'He couldn't possibly work out anything as complicated as faking a suicide to hide a murder,' said Brenda, her voice thick with worry.

'Could you, señora?'

'Me?' She stared at him, wide-eyed. 'For Heaven's sakel Everyone knows I can't think of anything more complicated than what to drink next.'

'I believe you are unkind to yourself.'

'And just what's that supposed to mean?' demanded Adamson, with a weak display of belligerence.

'That I feel certain the señora is far more clever than she wishes to show.'

'It's very sweet of you to say that,' she said, 'and I dearly wish it was true, but John would have disillusioned you. He used to get terribly angry because I couldn't understand anything complicated. But I've always preferred the fun things in life. I mean, Wagner's all right if you feel like examining your soul, but who wants to do that more than once? And why read books which don't end happily ever after? Otherwise it all gets too much like real life.' She stood up. 'Now you've made me feel all solemn and unhappy. So let's have a drink and cheer up.'

'Señora … ' began Alvarez.

'Come on now, stop being serious. I'm sure you can be a real sweetie if you relax. You've got kind of cuddly eyes. What are you going to drink — brandy? D'you know, I still haven't heard your Christian name! Isn't that incredible? What is it?'

'Enrique.'

'Adorable. It makes me think of the full moon on the bay. Names are so terribly important. Who can ever snuggle up to, and feel soulful with, an Adrian? But Enrique … It's warm and cosy and cuddly, like your eyes.'

'You are very kind, señora, but no matter how kind, I cannot forget I have come here to question Señor Adamson.'

She stared at him, hands on her hips, a fierce expression on her face. 'Then I think you're just a nasty block of ice.'

'That is a great pity.'

'I'm not sure I'm even going to give you a drink … But maybe I will. I suppose you can't really help it, it's just your job and you'd be a sweetie if you were allowed to be.' She crossed to the drinks table. 'Will you have a brandy?'

'Yes, please, señora.'

She searched for a clean glass amongst all the dirty ones beside the bottles.

Alvarez spoke to Adamson, putting his question with deliberate abruptness. 'When and where were you in trouble with the Spanish police?'

'Oh my God!' exclaimed Brenda, and dropped a glass which smashed.

'Who … who said I'd ever been in trouble with 'em?' muttered Adamson.

Alvarez waited.

'Don't you … ' began Brenda. Then she realized that nothing she could say or do would alter the situation and, shoulders slumped, she turned back and looked for another clean glass.

Adamson cleared his throat. 'I … I guess there was a bit of trouble once.'

'When?'

'About three years back.'

'Where?'

'Valencia.'

'What happened?'

'I was in a van that turned out to have a load of grass hidden away in it.'

'You are referring to marijuana?'

'Yeah.'

'Go on.'

'Four of us had been knocking around in Morocco for weeks in this Volks minibus. Then we sailed over to Valencia and the police and customs hit us like a ton of bloody bricks. They stripped the van out and found the stuff.'

'You were jailed?'

'They slung us into a stinking jail before we'd time to shout for help.'

'How did you get out? Drug smugglers in Spain usually get at least five years.'

'Me and the other two didn't know anything about it — that's dead straight. It was all Bruno's bloody silly fault. I could've told him, forget it, it's not worth the game in Spain. Bruno was level and told 'em it was all his idea, but at first they weren't interested. Then some bloke from our consulate came along and got us a lawyer and someone else got in touch with the place in Morocco where Bruno'd bought the grass whilst we were visiting friends fifty miles away and they said, sure, it was only Bruno who did the buying, In the end, the lawyer got us out of the nick. But not a word of apology.'

'How long were you inside?'

'Eight weeks and it seemed more like eight months.' Quite long enough to have made contact with a master forger. 'And that's all?'

'What more d'you want?'

'Is Bruno all right?'

'How should I know?'

'Haven't you been back to find out?'

'In my book, if a bloke's a bloody fool who gets his pals into trouble, he's got to learn to live with himself.'

He'd run, thought Alvarez with contempt, and had not stopped running until he'd reached the island. 'Now let me see your hands.'

'What for?'

'I wish to see if they are at all damaged.'

'Because of John being strangled? Look, mate, I told you, I didn't do him in.'

'Then your hands will surely be unmarked.'

Brenda handed Alvarez a brandy and Adamson a gin and tonic: she poured out a Ricard for herself. She sat down on the settee and looked from one to the other of the two men, worry twisting her very full mouth.

Alvarez drank, then put the glass down on the floor by the side of his chair, stood up, and crossed to Adamson's side. 'Let me see your hands.'

Very slowly, Adamson extended his hands. They shook. 'I've been boozing too much.'

The palms of Adamson's hands were unmarked. 'Turn your hands over, please, so that I may see their backs.' Once again, it was clear that the skin had suffered no damage within weeks. Alvarez returned to his chair.

Adamson lit a cigarette. 'Didn't I tell you? The trouble with you blokes is, you'll never believe anybody.'

'Perhaps in our job that is necessary. Señor, where were you on the twenty-first of July, a Wednesday?'

'He was with me,' said Brenda loudly. 'I told you that last time.'

'It would be much better if the señor answers me, señora.'

'I was with her,' said Adamson and a trace of his usual cockiness had returned to his voice.

'You are quite certain?'

'Couldn't be more certain.'

'Have you done much shooting?'

'He's never done any,' said Brenda.

'That's dead right. I don't know one end of a gun from the other. So I didn't stand that gun in his lap and pull the trigger and make it seem like he'd committed suicide.'

'Señor, it seems that the person who faked the suicide either knew nothing about guns or forgot what he did know.' Adamson was plainly shocked to discover that his vehement denial had been to his own disadvantage.

'Do you have a car, señora?'

She shook her head.

'Do you sometimes hire one?'

'If I need one.'

'From which firm?'

'The one along the road at the back of here.'

'Garage Llueso?'

'If that's its name.'

'Have you hired a car from there recently?'

'No.'

'And have you, señor?'

'No.'

Alvarez finished his drink. 'I think I have finished asking questions. Thank you for helping. Now all I need to do is to ask you, señor, to let me take your fingerprints.' He heard Brenda sharply draw in her breath.

'Do what?' demanded Adamson hoarsely.

'There was a print on the gun which I wish to identify.'

'It wasn't mine,' said Adamson, with certainty.

Brenda was clearly reassured by Adamson's answer. 'Come on, Steve, drain your glass. We're all waiting with our tongues hanging out.'

'I think, señora … ' Alvarez began.

'You're not going anywhere until you've had the other half.' She stood up, crossed the centre of the room to take his glass, and then went over to the sideboard. 'John always used to say that a one-drink man was basically untrustworthy because he wasn't one thing or the other.' As she poured out the drinks, she giggled.

'What's so funny?' demanded Adamson.

'That made me think of you, love,' she answered enigmatically.

She gave Alvarez back his glass, took Adamson's and returned to the sideboard. 'Bottoms up, Enrique. Or as an old boy-friend of mine used to say, "Here's to the health of your blood, if your health isn't bloody, your blood must be healthy ... " I'm sure I've gone wrong somewhere.'

'Like always,' muttered Adamson.

She giggled again. 'You know something? It kind of still makes sense the way round I had it.'

She had a remarkable habit, Alvarez thought, of twisting things round and yet still making sense.

*

Goldstein stood squarely in the centre of the sitting-room. He held his chin high and his shoulders ramrod straight. 'I wish to make it quite clear that I protest most vigorously at the inference which lies behind your words.'

'Perce, the inspector's only ... ' began Amanda.

'I shall speak to the British Consul. I will not be termed a criminal.'

'Señor,' said Alvarez, with grave patience, 'in an investigation of this nature ... '

'In England the police have the wit to confine their enquiries to those people who might conceivably have been guilty of the crime.'

'Señor, I merely ask that you show me your hands, give me your fingerprints, and account for your movements on the twenty-first of last month.'

'I am not a criminal.'

'Perce,' Amanda said, 'you're being rather difficult.' She looked appealingly at Alvarez, very frightened that he would be so irritated by her husband's rude boorishness that he would refer to what she had told him on his previous visit.

'We come from a country where it is every citizen's inalienable right to be as difficult as he pleases.'

'But, señor, you are now living in a country where it is every citizen's duty to help the police,' said Alvarez.

'Are you trying to threaten me?'

'Perce,' she said, 'for God's sake don't forget what could happen. Things are different out here.'

'Very different. There seems to be no differentiation made between criminal and gentleman. And stop calling me Perce.'

There was a silence, broken by Alvarez. 'May I now see your hands, please.'

'I act under protest. Is that quite clear?' Goldstein held out his hands.

The palms were smooth and the skin was unscarred. 'Would you turn your hands over, please.' The backs of the hands were equally unmarked.

'Does that satisfy you?'

'In this respect, thank you, yes. Now will you tell me, please, where you were on the twenty-first of last month.' Goldstein turned and stalked over to his desk, from which he picked up his diary. He turned back the pages. 'I went down to the Port in the morning.'

'On your own?'

'Yes.'

'Did you meet anyone who would be able to corroborate the fact that you had been there?'

'I have no record of such a meeting. Nor is it necessary. I went to the Port.'

'What about the afternoon?'

'I stayed in this house.'

'With your wife?'

'Do you wish to suggest I would have been here with anyone else?'

'Señor, I can clearly perceive that that is not possible.' Goldstein looked bleakly at Alvarez, but decided not to pursue the conversation.

Alvarez bent down and picked up his case. 'If I may put this on your desk and then take your fingerprints?'

'I suppose I cannot escape the miserable situation. But rest very assured that the consul will hear about it.'

*

Antonia lived with her parents on the outskirts of Llueso, in a small unmodernized cottage, rather pokey, often damp, which her mother kept scrupulously clean and tidy and of which she was as proud as if it had been a mansion.

Alvarez walked up the stone path to disturb a couple of hens which were scratching around in the dirt. There was a goat tethered under an algarroba tree and as he briefly watched it, assessing its shape and potentiality, he heard the grunts of a contented pig. This family still lived sensibly, he thought with approval, producing as much of their own food as possible and not becoming so lazy that they had to run every day to the nearest foodstore.

Antonia's mother was at the side of the house, weeding lettuces: bent double, she wielded a small, short-handled hoe with unvarying precision. When she saw him come round the house, she stood upright, pushed back her wide-brimmed straw hat which protected both her head and her neck from the sun, and called out: 'What do you want?'

'Is Señorita Antonia in?'

'She's cooking the meal.' She studied him. 'Who are you? What do you want?' she demanded, with some asperity.

'Inspector Alvarez, Cuerpo de Policia. But I have come only to ask your daughter something that's of no direct concern of hers,' he added reassuringly.

'Go on round to the back door, then.'

He went along the cinder path, past a lean-to from which came more pig grunts, a well, and a number of strings of tomatoes which had been prepared for drying, and came to the back door.

Antonia was making soup and the smell made him feel hungry. After introducing himself, he said: 'You work for the Meegans, the English couple in Ca'n Tizex?'

She nodded. She didn't fear him, as might an older person who had known how powerful the police had been in other times, but she was respectful and watchful.

'I want your help to try and discover what kind of people they really are. How would you describe them?'

'Describe them?' Her brow furrowed. 'I don't know anything, except they're foreigners. They're pleasant enough, but they waste a lot of food. I bring it back home and either we eat it or give it to the pig, so it does us some good.'

He leaned against the stone sink which was fed by a single cold water tap. 'How d'you reckon they get on together? All right — or do they fight a bit?'

'They're always rowing but I've never seen him hit her. And come to that, I reckon she's the kind of person who'd only let herself be hit once.'

He nodded. 'I know what you mean. Have they been rowing recently?'

She thought back. 'Not for a while, I suppose.'

'Then things have changed?'

She began to shred wild spinach with a large knife. 'I suppose they have. He used to go on and on at her and she'd shout back, but recently he's been all quiet and she's been all smiles and pleasant to him.'

'When d'you reckon the change came?'

She shrugged her shoulders. 'A week or two back,' she said, very vaguely.

'Have you any idea what they usually used to row about?'

'Not really.' She suddenly grinned slyly. 'But I'll bet you anything you like it was another man.'

'Why d'you reckon that?'

'The way he always got red in the face and shouted and she became all hoity-toity, like a woman does when she's trying to cover up.' She began to peel and then to chop an onion.

'Tell me something more. Have you noticed anything else about either of them recently? Has he looked as if he's been in any kind of a fight?'

She was surprised and for a few seconds she stopped chopping the onion. 'Here, that's odd, that is!'

'What is?'

'When you was talking about them fighting and I said he never hit her, I'd forgot the right old bruise he had on his cheek. I remember thinking at the time, had she laid into him?'

'How long ago?'

She shrugged her shoulders. 'Not very long. Much the same time as they stopped shouting at each other.'

He rubbed the lobe of his right ear.

*

In his office, Alvarez leaned back in the chair and put his feet up on the desk. For a time he stared at the shutters, partially opened to allow enough light into the room to prevent its being gloomy, then he removed his feet, leaned forward for the phone, checked what the number was and dialled the Institute of Forensic Pathology. He spoke to the professor's assistant and asked if it were conceivable that a man could be strangled without his tearing at the strangler's hands?

'It's like this, Inspector. When a bloke's being strangled it's a hundred to one he panics and when he panics he doesn't stop to think of hitting the strangler in the goolies or to bring his own hands up between the other's and jerk them away, he just claws at the wrists and arms. That's why in nearly every case where the victim isn't drugged or drunk, he tears the strangler's hands.'

'Suppose in this case there was a fight first and the strangler tied up Calvin's hands before strangling him?'

'You can forget that one. We checked under the skin of the wrists and there wasn't any bruising: the dead man didn't have his wrists bound.'

'But the skin under Calvin's nail quite definitely wasn't his own?'

'No way.'

'Shit!' said Alvarez. After saying goodbye, he rang off.

He poured himself out a drink and lit a cigarette, then heaved himself to his feet and went over to the window to open the shutters fully, flooding the room with sunlight. On the desk he laid out the sets of fingerprints he had taken and, using a magnifying glass, compared these with the unidentified print on the shotgun. None of them matched. He swore for the second time.

CHAPTER XVI

Superior Chief Salas rang at nine o'clock the following morning. He spoke with cold precision, lisping heavily to underline the fact that he was a native of Madrid and was only on the misbegotten island because duty held him there. 'Alvarez, I have received no general progress report in the murder case.'

That was logical, thought Alvarez: there had been no progress.

'You initially confuse a suicide with a murder, it is now two full days since you uncovered proof of murder, yet to date I have received no general progress report. Why not?'

Alvarez stared at the copy of *Ultima Hora* he had bought on his way in and he noticed the day was Friday the thirteenth. By Mallorquin tradition this was not an unlucky combination, but by British tradition it was — this case concerned the British. 'Señor, there are very many facets of the case which have had to be exhaustively investigated and I had no wish to send in any details before being quite certain … '

'I have not even received a report on the post mortem findings.'

Alvarez scratched his head. He reached down to the bottom drawer and brought out a bottle of brandy. With Salas on the phone and Friday the thirteenth on the calendar, a man needed something.

Salas sarcastically wondered if Inspector Alvarez even began to understand the urgency of the case — a foreigner murdered on the island, which relied on tourism for its prosperity. And had he somehow failed to appreciate the fact that the honour of the Spanish police was sharply involved? An honour which unfortunately appeared to be in very doubtful hands …

When the call was finally over, Alvarez slumped back in his chair and stared at his empty glass. Not a word of praise for uncovering the murder in the first instance. What a blunder it had been to uncover it! Why, he wondered resentfully, should he, who didn't give a twopenny damn if his name became completely forgotten by everyone in authority except the pay branch, be landed with a case which ensured his name was permanently before his superiors' notice? Surely there were inspectors by the score who would have been delighted to be faced with solving the insoluble, certain they would succeed and that success would lift them high … ?

Calvin had been murdered. Throttled. But the scene had been cleverly set to suggest suicide. The murderer, then, had not only to be a clever man with a mind which could look round corners, he also was either a very good forger or knew one such … But however clever, he had made mistakes — he had broken the gun to check the used cartridge and had not realized this would recock the gun, he had left a fingerprint on the stock. Several people were known to have motives for killing Calvin and these motives were either of a financial or an emotional nature. One of those suspects, then, undoubtedly should have been scratched on his arms and his prints should match the one on the stock. None of them had a scratched wrist, the prints of none of them matched. Then was there someone as yet unsuspected? Another jealous husband? Someone swindled by Calvin? Or had Collom hired a third person to kill Calvin?

He had never liked suppositions or theories, because in the main he distrusted them all. He was of a simple nature, the kind of person who looked at a spade and saw no more than a spade. Where did such simplicity get him now? Meegan had been bruised on the face, he was very worried about something and his wife was very worried about him. Adamson was a hyena of a man, prepared to live off a woman, who appeared to lack both the warped courage needed to murder and the clever mind needed to set the stage for a bogus suicide (but Señora Calvin was not the fool she made herself out to be). He had had direct contact with criminals, amongst whom there must have been at least one good forger. Goldstein was an icicle, a parody of a loving husband, and his wife was to be congratulated on finding a pleasanter bed elsewhere — but could an icicle warm up sufficiently to murder in the name of passion? Collom was a bear, friendly to look at, dangerous if aroused. But clever enough to have conceived the suicide … ?

Meegan was showing the kind of mental strain the murderer might be expected to suffer. And his wife clearly feared the worst. But he didn't fit the facts.

Alvarez poured himself out a second and larger brandy.

*

Meegan tried to find the words to type. They refused to come, as they had for so many days. People had often said to him how lucky he was to be able to write — he took his work with him, could live in the sun, didn't have to commute, didn't have to dress up and say yes-sir, no-sir, to anyone. But had any of those who'd envied him the slightest conception of what it was like to suffer all the mental strain of creating plus the additional bitter mental pain of knowing that what one was knocking one's brains out for was totally ephemeral and eminently forgettable? Had any of them an inkling of how exhausted the mind became after a very few hours of creative writing? Oh, for the simplicity of the life of the bank clerk commuter!

He heard a car squeak to a halt and identified the inspector's Seat and his hands began to sweat and shake. He heard a murmur of voices.

Helen came into the room. 'I'm sorry to bother you, Jim, but it's that detective again and he wants to talk to you.' She lowered her voice. 'Jim … you've got to … '

He interrupted her. 'Stop worrying. There's no need.'

She stepped up to his chair and took hold of his right shoulder and gripped him so hard that she hurt. Then, abruptly, she released him. 'He's going to have some coffee so I'll make it for all of us.' She turned and left.

He lit a cigarette, dragged the smoke down into his lungs, and tried to will his hands to stop shaking. After a couple of minutes, he stubbed out the cigarette. He left.

Alvarez was leafing through an art book on the low coffee table. He closed the book with care and then said: 'Good morning, señor. I have apologized to the señora for interrupting your work, but I am afraid it is necessary.'

'Has something happened, then?'

'I have to ask fresh questions … Señor, you own a Seat six hundred?'

'Yes.'

'Do you use it a lot?'

'My wife shops with it and I often take it out for a drive. When I can't get ideas for my books, it helps to potter about the roads.' He shrugged his shoulders. 'I can't explain why, but maybe the movement jogs my brain up just enough. I quite often get results.'

'In your travels, have you driven up the dirt track which leads off the Laraix road to the left, just past the bridge over the torrente? It goes right up into the foothills where, I was told, a German has built a very large house.'

'I've probably been along it sometime, but I can't remember a specific occasion.'

'Señor Calvin's finca is there.'

'I know.'

'Off this track is another and much smaller one which starts not far from Señor Calvin's house and winds half-way up the mountain. Perhaps you have also explored that?'

'No. I'd no idea it was there.'

'Nor had I, until an old shepherd told me about it. You are quite certain you have never driven up that small track in your Seat six hundred?'

'I've just said I am.'

'Then you will have no objection to my examining your car?'

'Examine it for what?'

'I noticed the track at one point passes through an unusual kind of soil. I would like to make certain that none of this soil has found its way on to the underside of your car.'

'For God's sake, don't you understand? I haven't been there.'

'Señor.' Alvarez gestured with his hands. 'Surely you will realize that I have to check everything? But nothing makes me happier than when I discover it is all exactly as I have been told it was.'

Meegan's voice rose. 'I'm not a liar. I've never been up that track.'

Helen hurried into the sitting-room from the kitchen. 'Would you like a biscuit with your coffee?' she asked Alvarez, her voice a shade breathless.

'Thank you, señora, that would be very nice,' he answered. What a wife, he thought admiringly, with what a sense of timing!

She picked up a pack of cigarettes. 'Will you have one? We smoke rather heavily out here because the cigarettes are so cheap. If we were back in England, we'd probably have to pack it in altogether.'

He was kind enough to go along with her, to let her chatter on inconsequentially, keeping the conversation away from her husband. Eventually, however, they heard the hissing sound of the espresso machine as the coffee was made and she was forced to return to the kitchen. As she passed Alvarez, she stared appealingly at him, but when she saw his look of compassion her own expression became one of resigned despair.

Alvarez spoke to Meegan. 'Señor, when I was last here I remember asking if you had recently been in any way physically hurt. You said you had not.'

Meegan stubbed out one cigarette and lit another. 'Well?'

'Was that quite correct? Did you not suffer some bruising on your face a short time ago?'

143

'What if I did?'

'Why did you not tell me when I asked about such matters?'

'Because it was immaterial.'

'Not necessarily, señor. As I explained to you, the man who throttled Señor Calvin must almost certainly have had injuries.'

'You were asking about scratches on the hands and my hands were unmarked.'

'I first asked about any form of injury, but perhaps we misunderstood each other. Now we can overcome that problem and you can tell me how you were bruised?'

'I ran into a door.'

'Whereabouts?'

'In this house.'

'Why did you do such a thing?'

'What's it matter, why? Haven't you ever run into a door in the dark?'

'Was there no electricity?'

'No.'

'What day was this? I will confirm with GESA that there was an electricity cut and everything will then be explained.'

He seemed quite unaware of the fact that his question had barbed hooks to it, thought Meegan, as he desperately tried to wriggle out of the corner he'd landed himself in. 'I didn't say there'd been a cut. All that happened was I didn't turn the light on. I didn't want to wake up my wife when I went to the bathroom.'

'Of course not. And you hit your face on … ?'

'The door. It made me see stars for a while.'

'I am sure it did.'

Helen returned to the room with a tray on which were mugs, sugar, milk, and an assortment of biscuits in a shallow earthenware bowl. Meegan spoke quickly, not certain how much she had heard of the conversation through the serving hatch. 'The inspector's been asking how I got that bruise on my cheek. I told him about walking into the bedroom door and seeing stars.'

She spoke lightly to the inspector. 'I've told Jim more than once that he sounds like a herd of elephants whenever he gets out of bed, so it doesn't make the slightest difference to my waking up whether he switches the light on or not. It's so silly to walk around in a pitch-black room. He could have hurt himself really badly.'

'Indeed he could have, señora.'

'I wonder why all you men are far too stubborn to take the slightest notice of your wives?'

Alvarez smiled. 'Perhaps, señora, we do not believe wives should ever be able to feel that important.'

She passed the coffee and biscuits, sat down, and carefully kept the conversation light and inconsequential.

Alvarez put his empty mug down on a coaster on the coffee-table. 'Señora, that was delicious coffee.'

'Have some more — there's plenty in the kitchen keeping warm.'

'Thank you, but I have so much work to do that I must leave now.' He stood up and turned to Meegan. 'Just before I go, señor, will you come outside with me whilst I examine the underneath of your car?'

'If you're determined. I tell you, though, I've never been up that track in our car.'

Alvarez shook hands with Helen. 'It has been a great pleasure, as always,' he said, with grave courtesy.

Meegan led the way outside and then lifted up the door of the garage, which was balanced with counterweights, to send sunshine spilling inside and over the white Seat 600. Alvarez studied the car, decided the sunshine wouldn't be enough and went over to his own car to return with a torch. Puffing slightly, he squeezed himself between car and wall, then got down on hands and knees. He switched on the torch and examined the underneath of the car, first from one side, then from the other. When he'd finished, he came out of the garage, brushed his hands together, pulled out a handkerchief and mopped his face and brow.

'So what have you found?' demanded Meegan.

'I am happy to say, señor, exactly what you told me I would find. Nothing.' He held out his hand. 'Thank you for all your assistance. You have been most helpful.'

He left and crossed to his car, climbed in, started the engine, and drove off.

Meegan watched the car disappear up the slip road and desperately tried to evaluate what thoughts had been going on behind that broad, heavy, sad-looking face. It was a hopeless task. The detective's expression had given nothing away. He walked slowly back past the shrubs and the rocks to the door and went inside.

Helen was standing in the middle of the sitting-room. 'Why did you lie to him?' she asked, her voice thin with worry. 'You told *me* you'd got the bruises from a branch.'

He crossed to the chest in which the drinks were kept.

'Jim, you've got to answer. Why did you tell him a pack of lies? What happened that you needed to lie? Where did you really get that bruise?'

'On a branch. But how could I ever have explained to him about wandering around, just trying to kick my brain into working? He'd never have understood and he'll get suspicious of anything he doesn't understand. So I told him something he could understand and accept.'

'But ... Jim, I don't believe you've told me the truth.'

'Now you're being crazy. Look, I ... '

'I think something terrible happened and you're frightened to tell me what. Don't you understand? There's nothing you could have done so terrible that I'd no longer want desperately to help you.'

'I ran into a branch.'

She turned away. There were tears in her eyes.

He lifted out a bottle of gin and went into the kitchen for a glass.

*

Dolores, Alvarez's cousin, said: 'Enrique, what's the matter with you?'

He looked across the supper-table at her, his thoughts still adrift and a puzzled expression on his face. 'What's that?'

Ramez, her husband, a round man, full of good humour, laughed. 'All that's the matter with him is he's got too much cognac under his belt.'

She ignored her husband. 'Enrique, you're hardly eating at all. Aren't you feeling very well?'

He looked down at his plate heaped high with Paella Valencia. 'I'm feeling fine.'

'I see. So perhaps you think the paella is no good?' Now there was a sharp tone to her voice.

He hastened to deny the possibility. 'How the devil could I think that? It's a paella fit for a king. Only my mother could ever have cooked one like this.'

Her pride restored, she smiled. She was a handsome woman, tall, with longish black hair which she kept drawn tightly back on her head so that it emphasized the ovalness of her face. 'My mother always said that your mother was a brilliant cook, especially when she had so little to cook with. But, Enrique, if it's good and you're not ill, why aren't you eating?'

'I was thinking.'

'If I was you, I'd pack that in,' said Ramez. 'That's the kind of thing what gets a bloke into trouble.'

She half turned. 'Then there's one load of trouble you'll never get into, isn't there?' She looked back at Alvarez. 'But what can you think about so hard that you don't eat?'

'It's the case I've got now. It's a pure bitch!'

'You mean the Englishman who was throttled?' Ramez was always enthusiastically interested, despite his cheerful nature, in any case of violence. 'What's happened now, then?'

'The trouble is, nothing's happened and I had the big man himself on the blower this morning, shouting for action. Action! Every time I take action, I hit my head on a bloody thick wall.'

'How d'you mean?'

'Look, it's like this: I'll give you just one example. The experts in Palma say the murderer must have scratches on his hands. So I check up on the suspects. Know what?'

'What?'

'No scratches on any of the bastards' hands.'

'Do try not to swear so much, Enrique,' said Dolores.

'What's the panic?' asked Ramez. 'The kids are in bed and can't hear.'

'Who's talking about the kids? I don't like hearing swearing all the time.'

'You!' He roared with laughter. 'Haven't you ever listened to yourself when something goes wrong?'

'Nonsense!'

Ramez spoke to Alvarez again. 'Look, I don't get it. If none of the blokes you looked over got their hands scratched, hasn't it just got to be someone else?'

'Yeah. Only there isn't anyone else I can find who could've wanted to knock him off.'

'What about ... '

'Give over,' said Dolores firmly. 'If you two go on like this the food'll be cold before you eat any more of it.'

'First things first,' said Alvarez. He refilled his glass with wine and then ate in silence, concentrating on enjoying the paella. And when he'd finished the very large helping she'd given him and she offered him a second one, he passed over his plate.

There was fruit on the table and they finished the meal with apples.

Ramez leaned back in his chair until he could reach round for a nearly full bottle of brandy. 'Give us your glass, Enrique.'

'Not too much, thanks.'

'Sure. Not more than half what's in the bottle.'

They drank in companionable silence, while Dolores cleared the table and washed up in the small, but well equipped, kitchen which overlooked a tiny courtyard, always bright with flowers.

At ten-thirty Alvarez, feeling mellow thanks to several brandies, said goodnight and left the other two to watch a very old film on television. He went upstairs, cleaned his teeth very carefully — he was very proud of his regular, white teeth — and in his bedroom changed into pyjama trousers. He pulled the sheet back and lay down. He yawned, began to read, yawned again, and decided it was ridiculous to continue to read so put the book down and switched off the light.

With the same irritating perversity he had recently suffered, sleep which had seemed about to overwhelm him now retreated at a gallop. He turned on one side, then the other, was finally seemingly about to drift off when a bead of sweat trickled down from his cheek and across his nose, making him swear as he brushed it away and dug his thumb into his face as he did so.

His mind insisted on concentrating on Superior Chief Salas. A cold fish of a man. What did he know about the problems of the case? It was so easy to sit on a well padded chair in Palma and moan about the lack of progress in Llueso. How much progress would he make if he were in direct charge of the case?

To hell with Salas, to hell with Calvin. What was so wrong with having an unsolved mystery? Instead of being disturbed, future tourists might well be intrigued and attracted by it. 'Ladies and gentlemen — not forgetting any English among you — that is the house owned by a man who was most foully murdered, yet whose murderer was never identified because he didn't have any scratches on his hands. So, ladies and gentlemen — and English people — somewhere in Llueso or the surrounding area there is a man who throttled the poor, unfortunate ... the smart, crooked Señor Calvin upon a rocky ledge on the side of the mountain where the view is God-possessed ...

Was it a white Seat 600 the shepherd had seen? A clapped-out, moving wreck of a Seat ... Old Seats never died, they simply rusted away.

Leopards never changed their spots. Why? Because they couldn't, that's why, even more than an elephant could pack its trunk. Pack its trunk … No, not very funny. Of course, cheetahs cheated and changed their spots … Wasn't a cheetah a kind of a leopard?

He was suddenly fully awake. He stared up at the ceiling, very faintly outlined by the light which crept up through the shutters, and heard a mosquito begin to manoeuvre around his head. If leopards didn't change their spots, what had happened to them when they were no longer spotty?

Sweet Jesus! he thought, why couldn't he stop thinking? Ramez had been right at supper — half the troubles of the world arose because people thought. But why had the faked suicide been staged up the side of a mountain, sheer enough to give a middle-aged bloke heart failure? Wasn't it possible it was because …

He switched on the bedside light and looked at his watch: nearly midnight. Surely the problem could wait until the morning? But even as he came to that decision that it could, he swivelled round on the bed and put his feet on the floor.

He dressed quickly, left the bedroom, and with the help of the landing light went quietly along to the stairs. He had reached the hall when there was a call from above.

'What's the matter?' demanded Dolores. 'Where are you going?'

'Out, to check on something.'

'At this time? Have you drunk too much cognac again?'

'I'm as sober as a judge.'

'That's not saying much, is it?'

'Look, something important suddenly occurred to me about the case when I was trying to get off to sleep and I must find out about it.'

'You're worried about your work at this time of the night? You can't be very well and that's why you didn't eat. Get back into bed and I'll … '

'I must go and check.'

'Stubborn bastard!' she exclaimed angrily, before returning to her bedroom.

He unlocked the front door and went out. His car was parked a few metres down the road and he climbed in behind the wheel, started the engine at the third attempt, and drove off.

There was little moon and the Laraix valley was dark, but not sufficiently dark completely to hide the mountains: their crests ranged away on either side to define and contain the valley and yet, paradoxically, mistily to enlarge it. The car's headlights picked out twisted algarroba trees, which seemed to writhe because of the play of shadows.

He parked in front of the gate of Ca'n Adeane, picked up a torch and his small, battered case from the front passenger seat, opened the gate, and walked along the path. Half-way to the house he stopped and picked a bunch of grapes: the grapes had ripened even in the few days since he had last tried them. At the house, he found the key in its usual hiding place and he unlocked the front door and went inside.

There was the scurrying noise of a mouse from above, then a flicker of sound from his right: when he swung the torch round, the beam outlined a gecko on the wall which froze in a curved position for a couple of seconds before fleeing across and down the wall with snake-like movements.

His best bet, he decided, was the bottles: Calvin would have handled them very frequently, but it was unlikely anyone else would have done. He went through into the sitting-room and in the torchlight the collection of objects seemed even more bizarre: the tiger's eyes glinted evilly and, absurdly, he ran the beam along its length to make certain it was still just a skin with a stuffed head. Not usually disturbed by atmosphere, he was glad to switch on the overhead light.

He put the case down on a convenient chair and took out of it a small jar of aluminium powder and a camel-hair brush. He painted the powder over the body of a whisky bottle and brought into existence a jumble of prints together with several individual ones: he checked the individual ones with the help of a magnifying glass. A bottle of gin, a bottle of vodka, and a bottle of rum, offered a large number of discernible prints and they were similar to the ones on the whisky bottle. There were at least three left-hand thumb prints and five right-hand ones. None of them matched the print which had been on the shotgun.

He stood up and whistled tunelessly. So there had been a very good reason for faking the suicide high up on the side of the mountain and that reason had nothing at all to do with the soul. On the contrary, it had to do with the leopard's spots.

CHAPTER XVII

Willis could not hide his nervousness and his manner was far from its usual breezy self. He kept twisting the ends of his flamboyant moustache. 'But how did you get hold of my name, that's what I want to know.'

'In the course of my investigations, señor,' said Alvarez placidly.

Willis was wearing a faded khaki bush shirt outside his even more faded light blue duck trousers. He absent-mindedly lifted the shirt and scratched his stomach. 'But I mean … ' He let go of the shirt.

'You were, I believe, in personal contact with Señor Breeden?'

'We met and discussed … business.'

'How did you like him?'

Willis seemed totally perplexed by the question. He'd been seated, but he suddenly came to his feet, crossed the tiled floor of the sitting-room, and stared out of the french windows, protected from the direct sun by the rush mats fixed to a wire trellis over the patio. 'Like him? Damn it, he wasn't really a bloke one liked.'

'Will you describe him to me, please.'

'Hell! I'm no good at that sort of caper.'

'I am sure, señor, you will be able to help me.'

Willis looked perplexedly at Alvarez. 'This bloke was … Well, it was like meeting a robot.'

'Do you mean he was cold in character?'

'Five minutes with him and you'd a bad case of frostbite. And crazy! You know how bloody hot it's been here? Well, he went around as if it was November in London. A suit. An ordinary, heavyweight suit in this heat.' Willis's manner gradually had become more confident. 'You know what was wrong with him, don't you? He reckoned he'd got to keep the flag flying amongst a load of chaps who'd gone native. You could read it in his manner. Silly bastard!'

'Is he a tall man?'

'Not really. Taller than the locals, of course, but then they're mostly chin-high to a midget … No offence meant, old man.'

'Of course not, señor. And is he young?'

'He's not young, no.'

'Old?'

'He's not old, either. He's one of those blokes you can't really tell. Call him middling.'

'Is he good-looking?'

'Not him.'

'What shape is his head? Round, square, oval?'

Willis thought. He went over to a chair and sat down. 'Like I said, I can't remember the details. I know exactly what I thought of him, but as for remembering what he looked like it's no good. He's just a blur. What's more, a blur I'm happy to forget.' His sense of uneasiness returned.

'Do you know where he was going after he went to Puerto Llueso?'

'I seem to remember he mentioned something about France, but to tell the truth I wasn't interested where he went so long as he cleared out from Playa Nueva bloody smartly.'

'Which part of France?'

'You do want to know some difficult things! Though hang on, something's stirring, I seem to remember … It was Nice, I reckon.'

'You've been a great help, señor.'

'Have I?' He was plainly surprised. 'Seems like most of the time it's been me not remembering. But honest to God, he's one of those blokes you just don't remember … How about a drink, eh? Talking always makes me thirsty. That reminds me. He didn't drink! Didn't drink! How can you hope to remember a bloke who doesn't drink?'

*

The Hotel Valencia in Puerto Llueso was on the sea front, to the east of the harbour: opposite it, on the sea side of the front road, was a large patio and pier, built out over the water, where the hotel guests could have breakfast, tea, and drinks. Part of the hotel was quite old, dating back to the time when the Port had been little more than a fishing village, part was new having been added in the past ten years. The reception desk was set in the old part, almost underneath one of three beautifully proportioned arches which spoke of Moorish influence.

When Alvarez entered the hotel a dozen guests, newly arrived by bus from the airport, were booking in and he waited, quite content to let the time flow by even though he was very curious to know whether he had at last discovered a little of the truth.

The last tourist, a stout woman who was bulging out of her cotton frock, handed over her passport and was given a room key. She left to cross over to the lifts which served the ten-storey new part of the hotel. Alvarez introduced himself to the receptionist, who pushed the pile of passports to one side, straightened up, and smiled a professionally wary smile. 'How can we help you, Inspector?'

'First off, by finding out who was on duty here on the twenty-first of last month.'

'Hang on, will you, and I'll make certain.' He moved along the counter and spoke to the second receptionist, who nodded and searched through a dog-eared ledger. After a while, he pointed out something with his forefinger. The elder receptionist returned along the counter. 'It's like I thought. I was on duty from nine in the morning until eight at night — Miguel was only with me in the afternoon.'

'Did you have any guests leaving that day — it was a Wednesday?'

'There'd have been a load out. Every Wednesday and Saturday they go, every Wednesday and Saturday, they come.' He sighed.

'Will you get hold of the list of people who left that Wednesday, please.'

'That's going to be difficult.'

'You're talking to someone who's been squeezed dry of the last drop of human sympathy.'

Alvarez lit a cigarette and propped himself up against the counter as he watched the people using the foyer. White faces, new arrivals: lobster faces, up to three days: tanned faces, the old hands. Strange to think that the sun had always been up in the sky but that only in the past twenty years of growth tourism had it proved to be so valuable an asset to the island. How did one explain the paradox of the desire for a skin darkened by the sun but not by birth?

The receptionist returned. 'I've found the list — damn near didn't, as a matter of fact. Another day and it would have been slung. The list is drawn up for the guests' arrival and then filed for their departure. That leaves us supposedly knowing where we are.'

'Give me a run-down on the procedure when people leave. When do they pay their bills for booze and all that sort of thing?'

'We draw up their bills the night before they're leaving and get 'em to pay these first thing in the morning. Anything they have to drink with lunch, or before it, they pay cash. That way, it makes it as difficult as possible for 'em to skip owing us anything when they go in the early afternoon.'

'Do they keep their rooms until they go?'

'They have to be out of them by eleven so as we can get 'em ready for the guests arriving in the evening. We tell them to bring their luggage down and store it over there, against the wall. It stays there until it's loaded in the bus. If there are any women with small kids, though, we let 'em stay on in the rooms: it's easier that way than having the kids crying all over the place.'

'What about lunch?'

'They sit at their usual tables. But like I said, they pay for the wine in cash instead of putting it on the bill.'

'Is everyone on a package tour?'

'Not everyone, but most. You know what it's like now — the bloke on the package tour gets his whole holiday for the same price as the independent bloke pays just for the fare.'

'If you've a bloke who isn't on the package, how does he go about paying his booze bill and what about his hotel room?'

'It's exactly the same routine because we can't alter things just for a few people. Pay the bill in the morning and if he's staying to lunch, cash for everything with the meal.'

'Fine. Now I'm in the picture, let's have a look at that list.' Alvarez was handed a typed list on which were ten names. The last one was T. C. Breaden. Someone had corrected, in ink, the a and changed it to a second e. 'I want to talk about Breeden. D'you remember him?'

The receptionist shook his head.

'Start trying.'

'Have a heart, Inspector. There are people coming and people going.'

'I know, it's like the Avenidas in the rush hour. But he was English, he dressed like a tailor's dummy, and he wasn't on a package tour. He was out here checking up on other English who'd moved money out of their country illegally.'

The receptionist thought for a while, began to shake his head, then suddenly checked himself. 'I do remember talk. Vicente said he'd heard an Englishman in one of the front bars shouting the odds about some bloke who was poking his nose into everybody else's business and someone else … ' He shook his head again. 'I don't know. With so many people, it's impossible.'

Alvarez put the list down on the counter. 'See this? Someone's altered the spelling of the name. Ten to one it was him because from the sound of things he was the kind of person who always wants everything just so.'

'That begins to ring a very small bell ... Yeah! There was a man who got all upset just because his name was spelled wrongly. I tried to tell him it didn't matter, but he wasn't having any — his name had to be exactly right.'

'Can you describe him?'

'Not a hope.'

'Was he in to lunch on the last Wednesday?'

'I don't know and, straight, there's no way of knowing now.'

'Did he pay his bill on Wednesday morning?'

'Must have done.'

'How can you be so certain?'

'We'd've marked him down on this list if he hadn't. If anyone welshes, we tell the police.' A trace of resentment crept into his voice. 'Not that you blokes ever do much about it.'

'You look like you've all got a long way to go before you starve. How was he travelling around the place? Had he a car?'

'You keep asking questions I couldn't answer in a thousand years ... Although now I do seem to remember something ... Keeps flitting around at the back of my mind ...' Alvarez produced a pack of cigarettes and offered it.

They smoked. The receptionist tapped on the top of the counter as he struggled to recapture the memory. All of a sudden he snapped his fingers. 'I'm sure it was him. I remember wondering why he was wearing a tie and coat when the temperature was like an oven. He'd rented a car from the airport and had told 'em he was returning it one day and now he wanted it for a couple more days. Asked me to ring the hire firm and tell 'em. And I said, just hang on to it and when you turn up at the airport they'll bill you quickly enough for the extra. But he was fussing away like mad so in the end I phoned ... D'you know, he never even bought me a drink!'

'Have you any idea what kind of a car it was?'

'None at all.'

'Or which firm he'd hired it from?'

The receptionist sighed yet again. 'Inspector, I'm on the desk seven days a week in the season. Sometimes we've a couple of dozen people coming ...'

'And a couple of dozen going. My heart bleeds for you.' Alvarez smiled. 'Change jobs for an easier life.'

The receptionist looked annoyed.

'Is there anything more you can tell me?'

'Not a thing.'

'If you should remember something fresh, give us a ring at Llueso.'

'Sure.'

Alvarez left and returned to his car which was parked caterwise to the right of the entrance into the hotel's patio. For a short time he appreciatively watched three young ladies who wore bikinis reduced to new minimum levels, then he started the engine, backed, and turned.

The drive to Palma took him well over the hour because there was heavy traffic in both directions, including a great number of coaches which reduced the standard of driving to an even lower level than usual, and in any case he had reached the mental age where he took great care of himself. Just before Pont d'Inca he turned off the Palma road and went cross-country to the motorway, then along to the airport.

He parked round the side of the main building — carefully saving the fifteen pesetas for the official car park — and stood by the car to watch a Jumbo jet take off. He wondered where it was going. England, France, Germany, Denmark? Countries he'd always wanted to visit: countries which, because he'd never travelled outside Spain, were for him invested with a glamour that was beyond correction by television or written description.

When the jet was well up in the sky, a bright ball of reflected sunlight which left behind slowly dispersing trails of dirt, he went into the departure hall which was filled with a seething mass of travellers who were struggling to overcome the problems of too few check-in points, a loudspeaker system designed for incomprehensibility, and a cafeteria too small and too expensive.

He went up to the balcony and along to the Iberia offices. 'I'd like some help,' he said to a harassed clerk, after he'd introduced himself.

'Oh God!'

'What's the matter? Busy?'

The clerk looked at Alvarez's heavy face and failed to make out whether he'd been joking or had asked the day's stupidest question. 'Couldn't you come back some other time?'

'Not a hope. Anyway, I've only one question. Did an Englishman named Thomas Breeden fly to the South of France on the twenty-first of July?'

'What flight number?'

'I've no idea.'

'I suppose,' said the clerk, with heavy sarcasm, 'you can at least be certain he flew with Iberia?'

'No, I can't.'

The clerk muttered something. 'Let's have the rest of the facts.'

'His destination may have been Nice.'

'That's all?'

'Yes.'

'You're not serious?'

'Quite serious.'

'But ... but ... Have you any idea how many flights there are out of this airport in a day by how many airlines?'

'Thankfully, no.'

'It's ... it's bloody impossible.'

'Remember the old adage: we can do anything, only the impossible takes a little longer. I'll come back later for the answers.'

Alvarez left, returned downstairs, and went to the far end of the building, past the international arrival hall, to the two kiosks used by the car-hire firms. He spoke to the clerk at the first one. 'Check your records, will you, and see if an Englishman called Breeden brought back a car on the twenty-first of July.'

'Sure.' The clerk left his seat and went over to the filing cabinet. He opened a folder and leafed through a number of forms, then brought one form across to the counter. 'Yep, he was with us. He checked in at three in the afternoon.'

'What kind of car did he have?'

'A Seat six hundred.'

'What was its colour?'

'Now you're really asking ... Hang on and I'll try and find out.' The clerk went back to the filing cabinet and pulled open the bottom drawer. After a while, he stood upright and returned. 'It was fawn, six months old, registration number, PM one-eight-two-five H.'

'I believe the car was held for longer than was originally booked. Did Breeden pay you in full?'

The clerk looked curiously at Alvarez. 'You seem to know quite a bit about this hire?'

'A bit but, as yet, not enough.'

'The hire charge was paid in full. Twelve thousand five hundred pesetas.'

'God's teeth! No wonder it's a popular business. Who dealt with him when he brought the car back and paid the bill?'

'The entries are in my writing, so I must have done.'

'But you can't actually remember?'

'No, I can't. We've been very busy ... '

'The curse of mankind! ... Let's see if I can start jogging your memory. This bloke was English and he dressed as if it were midwinter in the Arctic when the rest of us couldn't chuck off enough: suit, tie, woollen combs, for all I know. Like as not he was sweating buckets, but was still too damned stupid to take his coat and tie off.'

The clerk leaned against the counter and thought. He brushed the palm of his right hand over his smooth black hair. 'There was a bloke like you've just said — made me twice as hot just to look at him. I can remember thinking that if anyone had ever made life difficult for himself ... His shirt was so tight he couldn't leave the collar alone.'

'You're performing miracles. Now describe him.'

'What did he look like? No, it's no good, Inspector. I can remember the clothes, because they were so bloody stupid, but the face was just another face.'

'You can't say whether it was round, oval, square, long?'

'It's only those stupid clothes I can remember.'

'Will he have signed anything?'

'Not when he returned the car, provided it was undamaged. All the signing is done when a bloke picks up a car.'

'Did he talk to you much?'

'Hardly spoke, as near as I can remember. Half of our customers talk too much, the other half don't talk enough. Know what our boss says about the silent ones? Chat away gaily, bring verbal cheer to the customer's life ... How can you cheer up a bloke who just grunts because he's got a nagging wife and ulcers?'

'Offer him a pinch of arsenic and a glass of milk. Can you dredge up any overall impression of this bloke, even if you can't get specific?'

The clerk again smoothed his black hair. 'I'd say he was pretty nervous. Now don't start asking me why I say that because I don't know. I just remember I thought that at the time.'

'Ten to one, you're dead right.'

'And he was clumsy. You know, one of those blokes who's all elbows and knees. He knocked over that load of price lists, there, near your elbow, and when he went to put the box back, damned if he didn't drop it on the floor.' 'Sounds as clumsy as you can get. Was the box here, on the left?'

'That's it. It's always there — boss's orders. "If everything has its place, its place is known to everyone." Makes one want to puke!'

'How did he come to knock it over in the first place?'

'He was trying to give me the keys of the car.'

'With which hand?'

The clerk rocked back on his heels. 'You're right, you know! He was left-handed! That's how when he reached across he knocked the box over … Is that important?'

'Fairly important.'

'What's it all about?'

'A bit of a mix-up,' replied Alvarez vaguely. 'Well, thanks for all the help.'

He left and returned the length of the building and went into the cafeteria, built on the open plan so that the only division between it and the rest of the space was a long wrought-iron grille of elaborate design, and ordered a beer. The beer cost him so much he could not enjoy it.

He returned to Iberia's office upstairs.

'You're in luck,' said the clerk, as if he resented the fact. 'I've traced out Breeden. He flew Lufthansa to Nice — the plane goes on to Frankfurt.'

'What time?'

'Left here at four-ten.'

'Is it certain he was on the plane?'

'Sure. There was a full complement.'

'There was quite definitely a specific check on numbers?'

'That's what the airline says.'

Alvarez thanked him and left.

*

Alvarez had lunch at Llueso, eating the fixed meal at Ca'n Molin which cost him a hundred and fifty pesetas and was remarkably good. Afterwards, he had a brandy and a coffee at the Club Llueso. From there, he returned to his office. He sat behind his desk, belched, reached across for the telephone and dialled HQ in Palma. He asked to speak to communications.

'Get on to England, will you, and ask them for details concerning the present whereabouts of Thomas Breeden, an employee of the Bank of England, who was on this island until the twenty-first of July when he flew to Nice with Lufthansa at sixteen-ten hours.'

'Are you giving any reason for the request?'

'Not at this stage.'

'OK. Let's have the usual requisition form right away, will you?'

Alvarez rang off. He made a note that sooner or later he must send HQ a requisition form for the Telex message, then leaned back and thought that it was a long time since he'd had so busy a morning. He felt tired. He closed his eyes.

*

Palma rang just before eight o'clock that evening. 'We've heard from England, Inspector. And it seems you've really stirred something up. I'll read their Telexed message over to you. "Thomas Breeden checked in Hotel du Mail, Rue de Thermes, Nice, eighteen hundred hours, twenty-first July. Around twenty hundred hours, left hotel after asking whereabouts Rue Taillot and saying important appointment. Not seen again. Suitcase and briefcase, filled confidential documents, passport, travellers' cheques, left hotel room. Extensive enquiries. French police failed to trace his movements in Rue Taillot. Please advise if can assist enquiries." So that's that! Your bloke's taken off into the blue. You know what the French always say, don't you? *Cherchez la femme*. Ten to one it's a woman. Though come to think about it, if it was a woman, he'd surely not have left his money behind or he'd not even make first base with her.'

'It wasn't a woman.'

'What else gets a man real excited?'

'Money.'

'Yeah? Then why leave what money he's got in the hotel? ... Real Madrid's on the telly tomorrow, so you'd have to pay me a real bundle to go missing right now. D'you want to get back on to London?'

'Will you ask them for a full set of his fingerprints, if they can find them.'

'What's in the wind? D'you reckon to know where he's hiding out?'

'I'd say he's in the morgue.'

'In Nice? Surely even the French police would be bright enough … '

'Not there. Here, in Llueso.'

'He must have travelled far and fast, then?'

'Only after he was dead.'

CHAPTER XVIII

Superior Chief Salas was tall by Spanish standards and he was noticeably thin. He had a finely drawn, coldly handsome face. His eyes were a light grey, rather than blue, and his thin lips always became uneasy whenever he tried to smile.

He rested his elbows on his executive-size desk, joined the tips of his well manicured fingers together, and stared at Alvarez through the triangle formed by fingers and thumbs. There was a puzzled look on his face.

'The fingerprints came through from England late yesterday evening, señor,' said Alvarez. 'I've compared them with the prints of the dead man and they identify him as Breeden. So it was Calvin, impersonating Breeden, who flew to Nice. He booked in at the hotel, left Breeden's possessions in the hotel room, and vanished. That way, he made certain Breeden's disappearance appeared to take place in France and so in consequence all attempts to trace him would be concentrated there. Then no one would wonder about any deception back here in Mallorca.'

Salas gracefully lowered his hands. 'Inspector.' He paused. He began to study the air immediately above Alvarez's head. 'Inspector,' he said, for the second time, 'it has been my misfortune over the years to suffer in various cases, and on the part of my subordinates, slackness, carelessness, even total incompetence: but to the best of my knowledge this is the first time I have ever had to suffer slackness, carelessness and total incompetence inextricably mixed together in just one case.'

There was a silence. After a while Alvarez thought he ought to say something. 'The circumstances … '

'The circumstances defy reasonable explanation. Even the body was not discovered for weeks.'

'Señor, I had the house, the land around the house, and the fields around the land, searched. At the time, in view of the circumstances, it did not seem reasonable to order a still more extensive search.'

'The fact that the body was in none of those places should have been considered significant.'

'I'm afraid it merely reinforced my initial suspicion that it was a faked suicide and Calvin had slipped off because he found himself in a financial trap. I still don't think anyone could have been expected, lacking evidence, to call for the search to be extended right up to the rock shelf.'

'I have always expected — apparently mistakenly — a certain degree of imaginative intelligence on the part of my investigating officers.'

'But, señor ... '

'The kind of imaginative intelligence which would have immediately grasped the fact that the body had been placed where it had in order to increase the chance that time would work such havoc on the dead man's features that he would be unrecognizable.'

'But with a suicide note and half the head blown off ... '

'Did you not even once question yourself why the body was on the rock shelf?'

'Yes, señor. But initially I decided Calvin had chosen the place in order to fill his soul with peace and beauty for the last few moments of his life.'

'His soul!' murmured Superior Chief Salas with exquisite incredulity. 'And were you far too busy contemplating his soul to wonder what the true meaning obviously was of a gun which had been wiped clean of prints?'

'Later, as I've explained ... '

'Much later, I fear. Very, very much later.' Superior Chief Salas raised his hands again and joined his fingertips together. 'Have you, by any chance, gone on to consider the problem of where Calvin is now?'

'His description has been transmitted to all countries, via Interpol, asking for information. But the only photo of him I've been able to turn up is the one on his residencia and it's very poor. If he's careful, especially since he's almost certainly tucked away a fortune somewhere, I can't see much hope of uncovering him — ten to one, he's even had another identity lined up in somewhere like Switzerland in case of something like this ... '

'Inspector, I have always asked that my officers be optimistically enthusiastic, since this inevitably colours the spirit with which they conduct their investigations. I must confess, I am surprised to discover that your attitude is wholly one of pessimism. But perhaps this may explain how in this case almost all your time has been spent investigating the murder of a man who, it is finally discovered, was the murderer.'

There was another silence.

Superior Chief Salas lowered his hands and folded his arms across his chest. 'You have not, I believe, very long to serve in the force before reaching retiring age?'

'No, señor.'

'In the circumstances, this may be considered a fortunate coincidence.' He nodded briefly, to show that the interview was over.

Alvarez stood up. Although he had tried to look respectfully smart for the meeting, he was more than ever aware that his linen suit was rumpled, his bull neck was straining at his collar, and his tie was stained. In the eyes of the immaculate Superior Chief Salas, he must appear a wreck. He walked towards the door and his throat was so dry that he gloomily doubted if half a dozen brandies would be enough to moisten it.

*

Alvarez drove down to the Port on the Wednesday morning. A breeze, stronger than for several days, plus a certain amount of cloud, was keeping the temperature down. There were several yachts in the middle of the bay, while close inshore half a dozen Optimists were in the hands of boys who were being taught the rudiments of sailing. People were water-skiing and from time to time a speedboat started up with a harsh roar, drawing a skier upright and leaving behind a creaming wake. The beaches were packed with people sunbathing, many of whom would later have cause to regret the fact.

He parked his car and crossed the road towards the stairs leading up to Brenda Calvin's flat. A Mallorquin couple he knew were sitting outside the downstairs flat and he spoke briefly to them before going up. He crossed the balcony and knocked on the opened door.

'Come in,' Brenda shouted.

He stepped inside and as he did so she came into the sitting-room. She was wearing a pair of revealing pants and slip-slops.

'Good God!' she said, 'I thought you were Marge. She said she might be calling about now. What a laugh! I suppose I'd better go and put something on and be decent.'

He watched her return and suffered a fierce longing. To caress those breasts, even more magnificent than he had ever imagined them, to feel those cherry-tipped orbs nestling in the palms of his hands …

'There we are,' she said as she came back, wearing a shirt outside a pair of jeans. 'Do I look a bit more respectable now?' She laughed broadly. 'If you'd been ten seconds earlier, you'd've caught me starkers.'

If only he had not wasted his time talking to those people downstairs.

'Steve keeps telling me I shouldn't walk around skinny, but what the hell. I don't care — do you?'

He shook his head.

'As I'm always saying, one body's built exactly like another, so why all the fuss? ... Who d'you want to see this time? Me or Steve?'

'I came to have a word with you, señora.'

'Then sit down and make yourself at home. And I'm going to pretend it's twelve o'clock, so we can start drinking. John always said that moving the clock forward was the first sign of a devoted alcoholic, but all the time I know I'm putting it forward I can't see there's any danger. It's when I don't know I'll start worrying. Like Walter. He got really pickled and drove straight into the sea. He said his first thought was that it was raining really hard.' She went over to the sideboard, poured out two drinks, and took the glasses into the kitchen for ice. When she came back, she handed him one glass and went over to the settee and sat down. 'Here's mud in your eye.'

'Señora, I have to tell you about your husband.'

'Going to talk dirty, eh?'

'I have discovered that he is not dead after all.'

'But ... You told me ... ' She stared at him. 'Are you stewed right up to the gills?'

'No, señora.'

'Then for Christ's sake — you came here ... '

'He was the murderer.'

'Look, I know I'm stupid and can't really understand anything but my horoscope if it's good, but I don't reckon even Einstein could understand you now.'

He explained, as simply as he could, what had happened.

She fiddled with her glass. 'The cunning old bastard! Well, he is, isn't he? You've really got to take your hat off to him ... Oh, dear! I suppose that's being rather beastly to the poor man he killed. Do you think he was a nice man?'

'He was probably a very good man, but possibly not very nice to know. I am sure you would not have liked him very much, señora.'

'I'm glad. If someone you don't like gets killed, you can say how sorry you are without trouble. Otherwise you have to mean it and then things get so emotional. He always said I wasn't very good on the emotions — I was more physical. D'you think he was right?'

'I haven't really considered the matter, señora.'

'I can get emotional, of course. I think I'm going to get emotional now because I've just had a thought. Where is the bastard?'

'We've no idea. We are, of course, trying to find out, but ...' Alvarez shrugged his shoulders in a way of which Superior Chief Salas would have strongly disapproved.

'Then what about me?'

'You, señora?'

'When he was dead, I inherited everything on the island which was his. Now you say he's alive again. So doesn't that mean he's disinherited me?'

'In a way, I suppose it does.'

'Then he's left me in the deep end. The rotten swine. He's always said he's a rotten swine, but until now I've stuck up for him. I'm not going to do that again, I can tell you! I hope he ends up in trouble.'

'I am afraid your husband will end up in very serious trouble, if ever we find him.'

'Look — I don't want him in that serious trouble — that's overdoing it. Spain's still got that terrible garotte and I couldn't bear to think of his neck being squeezed and squeezed: he's got rather delicate skin.'

'I feel it is unlikely we shall ever catch him ... Señora, a thought occurs to me. You are still his wife.'

'I suppose I must be. It's a bit thick, that. I've only just got used to being his widow.'

'Then you can live in his house and if after a while he does not appear, you can go to court and ask for an allowance to be made out of whatever funds are his that are in this country.'

She drank. 'But that'll still leave bills to be paid because I'll bet he hasn't left any sort of a fortune here. Who's going to make up the difference?'

'Perhaps your friend, Señor Adamson, will be able to help you? If you cannot provide everything, he must surely provide something? Perhaps he could take a job?'

After a while, she smiled. 'D'you know, you're right! ... Am I going to have news for him when he gets back! I could hug you.'

The thought of a warm, enveloping hug from her set his pulse racing. He finished his drink and stood up. 'Señora, I hope all goes well for you.'

'It usually does, in the end, but I get a bit uptight at times. The trouble is, I'm the nervous type.'

Regretfully, he said goodbye and left.

At the corner of the eastern arm of the harbour, he bought himself a double cornet of ice-cream and when he'd finished that he strolled along the arm. Half-way along, he saw Collom in a boat, cleaning it down. He went to the edge of the arm and called out: 'I want a word.'

Collom stood upright, balancing himself with legs slightly apart. He wore only frayed cotton trousers and his bronzed torso was taut and muscular.

'Come ashore and get some news.'

'Come aboard and give it.'

Alvarez picked up the painter and pulled, slowly bringing the boat in until he could jump on to the after deck. He went for'd and stepped down into the large, open well. 'Getting ready to go out?'

'I'll be sailing this afternoon.'

'And what about tonight?'

'Depends where the fish are … Sit down, or you'll fall overboard and I'm not bloody well going to dive over and haul you out.'

Alvarez sat down on the starboard fore-and-aft thwart.

'I suppose you've got a thirst?'

'I'll not say no to a drink.'

Collom roared with laughter. 'By God, that's true, if every other word you've ever spoken is a bloody lie.' He went aft, past the engine, to the stern locker, above which was fixed the large gas-light used for night fishing. Out of the locker he brought an unopened bottle of brandy. 'Here you are.'

Alvarez unscrewed the cap, raised the bottle to his mouth, and drank heavily.

'You know something? You drink like a real man. Like I've said before, if you weren't a creeping policeman, I'd have you as crew.'

Alvarez lowered the bottle, rubbed the neck with the palm of his hand, and passed it back. 'If I weren't a creeping policeman and didn't mind the look of a jail, maybe I'd sail with you despite my sea-sickness.'

'Jail! There's not been a jail built to hold me,' Collom boasted before he drank.

'You can't always be lucky.'

'Why not? I'm lucky because I kick life around, I don't let it kick me. Make it respect me, that's what. And that's how I'll stay lucky.' He passed the bottle. 'What's the news that's got you all steamed up? Has someone dared to sell a fish without a government licence?'

'I've identified the murderer.'

'Taken you long enough. What's his name?'

'Calvin. It wasn't him up in the mountains, it was a man called Breeden whom he'd murdered to try and make it seem he was dead.'

'Trust you to make a balls-up.'

'Calvin is still very much alive.'

Collom's manner suddenly changed. His eyes were hard when he looked at Alvarez. 'Is he in Spain?' He began to pull at his beard.

'The last time he was heard of, he was in France.'

'Then I'd say he'll make certain he moves on and doesn't come near Spain again.'

'And I'd say the same. He struck me as a bloke who likes his neck the way it is.'

Collom relaxed. 'OK. So let's forget the bastard … Drink up, or the cognac'll go sour.'

They drank. They discussed fishing, brandy, women, and life. When the bottle was empty, Collom slung it into the harbour.

Alvarez stood up and the motion of the boat — the water was flat calm — caught him out, but with a bit of a struggle he managed to keep his feet. He went aft to the accompaniment of Collom's mocking laughter, stumbled up on to the after deck, pulled on the painter and scrambled ashore after being within a whisker of falling into the water. He waved at Collom, who'd begun to sing an obscene song, and walked with much dignity along to his car. Once behind the wheel, he lit a cigarette and smoked.

Later, and he had no idea how much later, he judged he was fit to drive. He backed, turned, and went along to the junction with the Llueso road, turning left on to that.

Amanda Goldstein opened the front door of Ca'n Setonia. 'Hullo. You want another word with us? Do come in. I'm afraid the place is in a bit of a muddle because Perce is busy altering his filing system, but you won't mind, will you?'

'Of course not, señora.'

The sitting-room was littered with files and papers and Goldstein was in the centre, bent double as he checked the contents of a file. 'It's the inspector, love, come to have a word.'

Goldstein picked up the file and stood upright. 'So I observe,' he said coldly.

'I've apologized for the mess.'

'There was no need to do so. In any case, it is not a mess. I am perfectly well aware of the order in which everything is placed.'

Alvarez said: 'I have come to tell you, señor, that the murdered man was not Calvin, but was Señor Breeden, from the Bank of England, who was investigating house purchases. Calvin murdered him and escaped the country dressed as Señor Breeden.'

'Good Heavens!' exclaimed Amanda.

Goldstein put the file down at his feet. He folded his arms in front of his chest. 'Are you confessing that your suspicions concerning me were totally unfounded?'

'Señor, you will understand ... '

'I understand that you were unpardonably impertinent in daring to believe I could have had anything to do with his murder. I naturally have not the slightest intention of forgetting such behaviour merely because you have at last had the grace to come to apologize. The British Consul will receive the fullest report from me.'

'Señor, I had to ... '

'I am totally uninterested in any excuses you might try to make.'

Amanda said nervously. 'Perce, don't you think you ... '

'Will you please not refer to me as Perce.'

Alvarez left. She followed him into the hall and as he slid back the lock of the front door, she murmured: 'I'm sorry he's like that.'

'Señora, it is of no matter.'

'And please don't worry about the consul. Perce went and complained and the consul told him not to be so stupid. That's why he's just been even more pompous than usual.'

He smiled, said goodbye, then went out to his car. As he drove down the hill to the Cala Roig road, he checked on the time. He ought, he thought, to call on the Meegans, but it wasn't long to lunch-time.

*

The late afternoon sunshine was cutting a wide swathe through the sitting-room of Ca'n Tizex when Meegan followed Alvarez into it. Alvarez sat and then noticed how Helen had begun to fidget with the buckle of the belt of her dress. It made him feel warmly benevolent, like a favourite uncle, to think that with a few words he was going to strip away all her fears.

'Señor, I have hurried here to tell you something very important. I have identified the murderer.'

Meegan, who had been about to sit on the settee, stood very still and Helen drew in her breath with an audible hiss that sounded like pain.

When he saw her pitiful state of tension, Alvarez was sharply annoyed with himself for that moment of dramatic pause. He hurriedly said: 'The murderer was Calvin and the murdered man was Señor Breeden. I am afraid that it has taken me a little time to discover the true facts of the case. I apologize to you.'

Meegan sat down heavily.

'You … you mean … ' Helen stared at him.

'Señora, any suspicions I may have had were utterly wrong. No one but Calvin was concerned in the murder.'

'Dear God!' She put her hand to her throat. 'Does anyone mind if I cry?'

Meegan jumped to his feet and crossed to her chair. He held her tightly against him. 'I'm afraid Helen thought …'

Alvarez interrupted him. 'Señor, other people's thoughts should always be kept private. I am truly sorry I had to question you in the manner I did, but it was my job. It has also been my job to come here now, to tell you the truth, but this has been a job I have greatly liked.'

Helen held on to her husband's hand as she said: 'I think you're a very wonderful man.'

Alvarez, to his dismay, felt himself blush.

'This calls for a drink,' said Meegan. 'Lots of drinks.'

'I think, señor, I had better not drink anything.'

'Why ever not?' she demanded. 'Not drink now? That's impossible. You've got to help celebrate.'

'Señora, this morning I confess I celebrated a little too well, though quite what I was celebrating was never clear.'

'Then you need a large hair of the dog which bit you. Jim, hurry up with a brandy on the rocks before he runs away.'

'There is little fear of that,' murmured Alvarez. 'If I ran anywhere in my present state, I fear I should suffer alarmingly.'

*

Helen watched the dented, rusting Seat 600 rattle away up the slip road. She turned. 'Jim, may I have another drink?'

'Why on earth ask me if you may?'

'I don't know, really. Or maybe I do. Perhaps I was hoping you'd say I'd had enough already. Then I could tell myself I needed Dutch courage to go ahead, but you'd refused me any so I could keep quiet.'

Meegan spoke in a strained voice. 'To go ahead with what?'

'You know as well as I do.'

He didn't answer her, but led the way back inside. 'What d'you want to drink?'

'I'll stick to vermouth. My mother always warned me against mixing my drinks or some nasty man would try to take advantage of me.'

As he poured out two drinks, she sat. He crossed past the fireplace and handed her a glass. 'Wouldn't it be better if we … '

'We've got to have it out, here and now. I must know why you were so scared. Where were you on the Wednesday? Why didn't you get back until God knows what time of the night? Where did you get that bruise which you kept on lying about?'

He drank.

'We've had our troubles, God knows! We've had arguments that have turned into rows because we've both been silly when we ought to have been living a happy life. Then I was the prize idiot on the island when I decided that if you were going to be bloody-minded, I was going to enjoy myself so I encouraged John. But when it came to the final crunch, I discovered that I hated what I was doing because I loved you, however nasty the rows … Jim, there's no need to tell me everything, but you met your own crunch, didn't you?'

He stared at her for a moment, his expression twisted.

'Because I'd been such a bloody fool, you decided to get your own back on me. You went out with another woman?'

After a while he nodded.

'What happened?' she asked, almost in a whisper.

'I discovered you meant far more to me than the rest of the world put together.'

'Was … was she someone I know?'

'I think you do.'

She lit a cigarette with fingers that shook slightly. 'You think? Or you know?'

'Just think.'

'Is she pretty?'

'So-so.'

'Prettier than me?'

'No.'

'But passionate?'

'She reckons she is.'

'And what do you reckon?'

'I'm not a very good judge.'

'Does she love you?'

'No.'

'You sound very certain of that?'

'I am. I thought you said there was no need to tell you everything?'

'Was it purely a physical attraction?'

'Yes.'

'And you weren't emotionally involved?'

'No.'

'The bruise. Things were getting very physical?'

'According to her, not physical enough.'

'What d'you mean?'

'I mean that, like you, I discovered I hated what I was doing.'

'But … but being a man you had to do it?'

'No. That's why I was clouted.'

'You … She hit you because you wouldn't tup her?'

'That's right. At the last moment, I refused. Sounds bloody silly, doesn't it?'

'Jim, it sounds like the most wonderful news I've ever had. Just think. Neither of us cut out for adultery! That must make us unique on the island … D'you know why I needed another drink? Because I was certain I had to find the strength to forgive you for bedding another woman. And then I was going to need another drink to stop trying to imagine who she was so I could rip her eyes out. Why wouldn't you tell me all this, instead of making me so scared that you'd something to do with John's death?'

'I was terrified you'd leave me if you knew about the other woman. But when you were scared I might be a murderer, you came much closer to me than we'd ever been before.'

'Jim, my darling, hurry up and finish your drink and come and kiss me and don't stop kissing me until tomorrow.'

He finished his drink and went over to her.

*

Alvarez lay on his bed and stared up at the ceiling, lit by the bedside light. There wasn't a shadow of doubt, life, despite everything, was good. There might be Goldsteins in the world but, far, far more important, there were also women who suddenly lost the fears which had been choking them and then they looked at one with an expression of such dazzling relief, such overwhelming joy, that one was offered a tiny window into Heaven.

If Juana-Maria could walk the earth again, she would look at him like that. Then he smiled sadly. Or would she? Wouldn't she see a paunchy, middle-aged man whom life had almost passed by and wouldn't her smile be wistful, not ecstatic?

He switched off the light and turned on his side. And as he prepared to sleep, he suddenly thought that a left-handed man impersonating a right-handed man wouldn't necessarily look clumsy: but a right-handed man impersonating a left-handed man impersonating a right-handed man inevitably must do.

CHAPTER XIX

Alvarez entered the Guardia post, grunted an ill-tempered answer to a bright good morning from a corporal, and went up to his room. He slammed the door shut, opened one of the shutters, and then slumped down behind his desk.

Contrary to what he had decided the previous evening, life was a bitch. How could he destroy the light in a woman's eyes? It would be as if he were the driver of the car which had pinned Juana-Maria against the wall, killing her, so that all light, and even all terror, fled from her eyes.

He swore. Collom was right and he wasn't born to be a policeman. He distinguished law from justice, believed unhappiness to be a serious crime, and was forever becoming emotionally involved in the lives of other people.

Sweet Mary, if only … But 'if onlys' belonged to the world of children. He picked up the telephone receiver and dialled. When the call was answered, he said: 'Señor, I am very sorry to disturb you once again, but there is a point I must examine before I make my report to Palma. So will you please come right away to my offlce at the Guardia post?'

After ringing off, he lit a cigarette. He drummed on the table with his fingers. He knew exactly how Juana-Maria would look at him now, with her liquid eyes which translated emotion into statements.

*

There was a brief knock on the door and a Guard showed Meegan into the office.

Alvarez stood up and shook hands. 'Good morning, señor. I am most grateful that you have come along. Can I offer you coffee?'

'Thanks, but I had some before I came out.' Meegan spoke abruptly.

'I think that perhaps you were very wise. The coffee here is rather peculiar.' Alvarez nodded at the Guard, who left and closed the door behind him. 'Please sit down, señor. The chair by your side is not as unsafe as it looks.'

Meegan sat down. 'What's … what's suddenly cropped up?'

'Señor, it is a matter of a nature which I thought was best discussed solely between you and me. Will you tell me, please, exactly how you received the bruise to your face?'

'You want to talk about that!' Meegan managed to smile. 'Then I can only admire your sense of discretion in asking me here. But as a matter of fact you needn't have bothered because after you'd gone yesterday I confessed the truth to Helen.'

'What truth was it that you confessed?'

'That the bruising came from a woman.'

'May I hear the circumstances?'

'I was fool enough to play hard and loose with a woman and we ended up stripped and ready for action. She was more than willing, I suddenly discovered I wasn't. That got her really furious and she let rip with everything she'd got.'

'She sounds a very passionate woman.'

'She is.'

'You know, señor, it was apparently an extensive bruise.'

'She has a great right hook.'

'I feel that few men would be able to resist so formidable a lady when events have reached a certain point.'

'God knows how I did!'

'You did not tell your wife the truth until last night?'

'I was too scared stiff that she'd be so sick and angry she'd leave me.'

'Leave you because you had resisted this woman?'

'Because she couldn't and wouldn't believe I had resisted.'

'But, señor — and forgive me for recalling the fact — the señora had been in a somewhat similar situation and she had resisted: would she not have had great sympathy and understanding?'

'I suppose I just wasn't thinking straight. I was far too scared of losing her.'

'So scared that you were careless that others might believe you had received the bruises in the course of murder?'

'I knew I hadn't murdered Calvin. On the other hand, I knew I had been with this woman.'

'Will you please give me her name?'

'No.'

'Why not?'

'It's all over and done with and best forgotten.'

'But she will be able to corroborate your story.'

'What's it matter whether, or not, it's corroborated? Calvin murdered Breeden and skipped off to France and that's it.'

'Unfortunately, now I am not so certain.'

Meegan's face whitened. 'Not so certain about what?'

'That Calvin reached France.'

'It's you who told me he had.'

Alvarez pushed a pack of cigarettes across the desk. Meegan, his actions suddenly woolly, took a cigarette: Alvarez struck a match for both of them.

'Señor, there have been one or two points in this case which have caused me worry and although I finally decided I had found answers, now it seems to me that those answers could be wrong … You are right-handed, are you not?'

'Yes.'

'Calvin was left-handed.'

'So?'

'Let me explain. Señor Breeden hired a car from one of the firms which work at the airport. I went along there and questioned the clerk. By then I knew it was not Señor Breeden who had returned the car and I thought I knew that it was Calvin who had. The clerk told me how clumsy the man was and how when he'd been handing back the keys with his left hand, he'd knocked over a box because he'd brought his hand across himself. Does that suggest anything to you, señor?'

'Merely that he was left-handed,' replied Meegan, trying to speak facetiously.

'A left-handed person doesn't normally appear clumsy. Why should he, since he is behaving naturally? What happens is that his left-handedness is only noticeable — not necessarily because it appears clumsy — when he's writing, playing a game, or something like that. Furthermore, left-handed people tend to use their right hand for many things so that to some extent they become ambidextrous. So if a left-handed man were impersonating a right-handed man returning a hired car, unless he had to write there is no reason to suppose he would appear clumsy in his actions … Calvin would have done all he could to appear naturally right-handed. And he would know not to pass the keys across his body with his left hand as then he would be offering them to the clerk's left hand.

'But suppose the man was not Calvin, but someone naturally right-handed who was impersonating Calvin impersonating Breeden. Then he would try to be certain that if enquiries were ever made it would become obvious that the man who had returned the keys had been left-handed. So this third person acted left-handedly and immediately appeared, and was, clumsy, because what right-handed man ever bothers to exercise his left hand? Again, acting instinctively, he passed the keys across his body as he had always done. Forgetting that he was now acting as left-handed.'

'You're making a mountain out of a mole-cast. Calvin was just plain scared. And scared men become clumsy.'

'Perhaps I would agree if the scene at the airport was my only query. But there are others.' Alvarez stubbed out his cigarette. 'Señor , was it not you at the airport, impersonating Calvin impersonating Señor Breeden?'

'That's bloody daft. I was …'

'Please listen. When I saw the body I was puzzled as to why it was right up there on the rocky ledge and why the gun did not eject, since the ejector seemed to be working. Eventually, I reached the answer to the first problem: Calvin had put the body there to let time and nature destroy the features completely. When I had that answer I assumed, because I am a man who prefers the simple to the complicated, that Calvin had been careless with the gun: but later, much later, I recalled to my mind that Calvin was undoubtedly very clever and although clever men make mistakes, they do not make them often in important matters. When I thought that, I also began to think of a third person on the rock shelf. Was it this third man who, knowing nothing about guns, inadvertently broke it, found the cartridge was ejected, replaced the cartridge and closed the gun, not realizing about the ejector and the cocking mechanism?

'There was the single print of Calvin's on the gun which had been wiped clear (though not completely) and then imprinted with Señor Breeden's prints. Calvin would never have wiped the gun clean. He would want both his own prints and Señor Breeden's on the gun. Then if comparisons should be made — which he believed and hoped to be unlikely — the dead man's prints would appear on the gun, or prints found in the house would be duplicated on the gun, suggesting in either case that the dead man was Calvin and that recently some friend of his had been using the gun. Only a cross check between the dead man's prints and prints in the house would show a meaningful discrepancy. But to leave a single print which must immediately draw attention to itself and raise questions …

'There was the light-coloured Seat which was seen to drive up the track. Although there was never proof it was connected with the murder, I had to assume it was. And recently I asked myself would Calvin, after all that planning, have driven Señor Breeden's car up the track, knowing there are always watching eyes in the country? Or was it the third person in Señor Breeden's car or his own car?

'There was the flesh under the nail of the dead man. The experts in Palma said that whilst he was being strangled, the victim had scratched his murderer's wrists. I could find no wrists which were scratched … '

'Of course you couldn't. It was Calvin's wrists which were scratched.'

'Indeed. But I have again spoken to the clerk at the airport and he does not think that the wrists of the man who returned the car bore scratches.'

'Doesn't *think*?'

'Señor, he refuses to be certain, he is only very nearly certain … But what I was going to say was that the only injury I discovered on anyone was the bruising to your face.'

'And I've told you where that came from.'

'So now you tell me the lady's name and where she lives and I will speak with her and she will be able to convince me I have been wrong again in many of my thoughts.'

'I … I'm not going to drag her into this.'

'I admire your attitude, but I think it is not very advisable. Señor, have you considered closely? I can take you to the airport to meet the clerk and I can ask him, "Do you recognize this man?" Or I can take you to the Hotel Valencia in the Puerto and ask the staff. Or I can take you to meet the crew of the Lufthansa plane which left Palma at ten minutes past four in the afternoon … '

'I couldn't possibly travel to France as Breeden. There's the passport … '

'That interested me. But I discovered it is not so very difficult, especially for an Englishman, in the height of the tourist season, to travel on someone else's passport. To begin with, I looked at an English passport and I wondered. The written description doesn't matter, unless it is immediately obvious that the description cannot be the person — the official who examines the passport has perhaps hundreds more to look at and all he wants to know is if the name is on the proscribed list: and even though you, Calvin, and Señor Breeden, could never be mistaken for each other when seen, your descriptions are not too dissimilar. So it is the photograph which should be the trouble. But I learned something. Because the back of the photograph has a shiny surface, after a time it can quite simply be pulled away from the page. Either the English do not bother to use paste which prevents this, or with a shiny back it cannot be prevented. So all the Englishman had to do was to peel off the photo of Señor Breeden and substitute his own — which had to be of similar size. Perhaps the impressed stamp of the Foreign Office seal was not in line, but would a harassed, sweating, irritated immigration or emigration officer, dealing with a foreigner, ever notice the event? Of course not.

'When the Englishman was in France, he removed his photo and replaced Señor Breeden's. Everything was now in order. If Señor Breeden's passport should one day be examined very carefully — and why should it? — it will be noticed that the photo has been removed and then been replaced. But who is to say whether it did not come loose and it was Señor Breeden who replaced it?

'The Englishman replaced the photo in his own passport and returned to Palma. On the plane, he will have been asked to fill in an immigration form or card. Perhaps he didn't bother, but presented his passport to the immigration official and pretended not to understand his request for the card. Did the tired, harassed, sweating officer worry too much when there was a long queue of people waiting and planes landing all the time to bring more queues? ... I will tell you. He did not worry. He shrugged his shoulders and waved the Englishman through. Thus there is no record of his ever having been out of the country, since these days no passport is stamped in Palma unless the traveller asks.'

'The whole of that's supposition. I tell you, I haven't been off the island since ... '

'Señor, listen very carefully to me. Your señora says she was with you all day and the night of Wednesday — so far, I have not tried to find out if she is quite correct. But far more important, if I take you to meet the clerk at the airport, the staff of the aeroplane, or the staff at the hotel, everything must become official.'

There was a silence.

Meegan ran his tongue along his lips. 'I don't understand what you mean by that.'

'I mean that then I can no longer use my discretion.'

'But ... '

'Tell me the truth, now. Sometimes, señor, one has to trust — even in defiance of logic.'

Meegan still hesitated, but then he looked at the heavy, square, lumpy, peasant face and saw only kindness. 'I … ' He stopped, swallowed heavily, resumed speaking in a harsh voice. 'I had to know about Helen and John, one way or the other, once and for all. My bloody imagination was mentally crucifying me. She'd taken the car, so I cycled. That's why he didn't hear me arrive. Our car wasn't there, but another Seat six hundred was. I'd reached the stage where I just immediately thought Helen had left our car somewhere and hired another so that she could move around without being recognized. I barged into the house, found no one downstairs, heard a noise from upstairs, and ran up …

'John was dressed in a dark suit and a tie. At first, that meant nothing. All I was concerned about was … The bed was empty and made up. I was feeling like someone who meets a miracle but can't quite bring himself to accept the fact in case it vanishes, when John shouted and came forward suddenly, kicking over a suitcase. The name "Breeden" was on the lid and that's when I suddenly wondered why John was wearing the suit. He obviously assumed I'd guessed the lot. He said I'd chosen a hell of a time to arrive, but would a million pesetas square things. I gawped at him and he became excited and told me there was no need to take fright: he'd dropped Breeden's body up on the ledge and made it look like it was his own body and he'd committed suicide. He was going to fly as Breeden to Nice and then let Breeden disappear. In one week's time I'd get a cheque on a Swiss bank for the equivalent of a million pesetas. I was about to discover that silence really could be golden.

'I went on gawping at him. I just couldn't accept the fact that he'd committed a murder. But when he raised the offer to a million and a half, I had to believe. I felt absolutely sick. I'd known John was unscrupulous, but I'd always thought it was a carefree, Robin Hood kind of attitude. Now, he was casually admitting murder …

'He saw I was really horrified and realized I wasn't going to take the offer. Suddenly he picked up a very thick piece of bamboo and came at me like an express train: God knows how I managed to avoid most of the first blow — I just got a crack on the cheek. Then he had another swing, tripped over the suitcase, hit his head on an antique dresser, and began to stagger around the place. He'd dropped the stick and I made a grab for it a split second before he recovered enough to do the same. I hit him as hard as I could and he went down like a sack of potatoes. Christ, it was ghastly! I tried to get him to come round, but after a bit I had to accept he was dead.

'First off, I naturally decided to call the police. But then I panicked when I tried to work out how I'd look — frantically jealous because of my wife, unable to *prove* I'd acted in self-defence, perhaps even unable to *prove* I hadn't had a hand in killing Breeden ... '

Alvarez spoke. 'Indeed, señor, you have correctly mentioned some of the problems. Always, if the truth is unusual, people try to disbelieve it because they wish for the normal. That is one of the reasons why justice may be overwhelmed by the law: another is that laws must live by laws and so they have limits beyond which all is black, although for one particular man it may be white.' His tone became uncertain. 'Perhaps I make myself sound very pompous? I do not wish to be pompous, but just to express what I feel ... Señor, the law can take a very long time and then life becomes most unfortunate for someone who is in a hurry because his wife is tortured by fear. I do not answer your question because it is one I have not asked myself. Why not? Because I am becoming an old man. Unlike the youngsters of today, I can remember when a woman's honour was more honoured than life and a man would kill anyone who cast so much as a shadow on such honour ... Calvin deserved to die at the hands of many men. You, señor, were the first man of honour, as we know honour on this island. So do not bother with details, except, as a matter of interest to me, to tell me what happened afterwards.'

Meegan stared at Alvarez for several seconds, his face expressing fear, tortured doubt, and the first stirrings of hope. In a croaky voice, he said: 'Because my job's writing books, I've a hell of an imagination. It worked at full pressure right then and I saw that if I carried out John's plan, everything could be OK for me. But first I had to go up to Breeden — if by chance he was still alive and could be helped, I wasn't doing anything but calling help. I used his Seat to drive up the mountain path which Helen had told me about — ironically because John had taken her for a walk part way up it.

'When I saw Breeden I knew that logically he couldn't begin to be alive, but emotionally I still had to make certain. I moved the gun — it opened and ejected — and felt Breeden's heart, then his pulse. When I was finally satisfied, I replaced the cartridge in the gun, wiped it clear of prints, tried to stick Breeden's prints on it, then stuffed it back into his arms.

'I stuck Calvin's body into a blanket and managed to wedge it into the car, drove back home — praying Helen was still out — and grabbed my passport.

'I went way up into the mountains, beyond Laraix, and found an overgrown dirt track that obviously wasn't being used and carried on along it for half a kilometre. Then I pushed the body out into the bush. I reckon there's not a house within five kilometres.

'I switched photos in the passports, drove to the airport and handed in the car, caught the plane to Nice. After checking in at the hotel and leaving Breeden's passport — with his photo back in it — I tried to fly straight back, but in the end had to go to Cannes where I caught a very late plane on charter which had a spare seat. The airline girl sold it to me for so little I suppose it was illegal and she was making herself some pocket-money.

'When I got home, Helen was in a hell of a state. I made up a story, which she didn't believe. Since then I've been sweating it out and nearly going crazy in the process ... What's going to happen to me now?'

'Señor, I knew a young woman once who looked at me as your wife has looked at you and the look in a woman's eyes can be more precious than diamonds. But the past is gone. The future is all that matters.' Alvarez stood up and held out his hand. 'Be very kind to her, señor.'

Meegan, as if in a dream, shook hands. He went to speak, saw the look on Alvarez's face and turned and left.

As the door shut, Alvarez sat down. He felt sad enough to weep. Instead of that, he brought out the bottle of brandy and poured himself a glassful.

*

As Meegan braked to a halt in the turning-circle, Helen came out of the house and ran to the car. She pulled open the driving door. 'What was it? What did he want?'

He climbed out and put his arm round her. 'I told you there was no need to panic. All he wanted was to see if I could help him tie up a few loose ends. And also to tell me that the light in a woman's eyes can be more precious than diamonds.'

'What ... what an extraordinary thing to say.'

'He's a simply extraordinary man.' He kissed her. Then together they walked towards the house.

Printed in Great Britain
by Amazon

66748462R00109